Nanny McPhee

THE COLLECTED TALES OF
NURSE MATILDA

by Christianna Brand
illustrated by Edward Ardizzone

BLOOMSBURY
CHILDREN'S
BOOKS

BLOOMSBURY

NURSE MATILDA
First published in 1964 by The Brockhampton Press Ltd
Text copyright © 1964 Christianna Brand
Illustrations copyright © 1964 Edward Ardizzone

NURSE MATILDA GOES TO TOWN
First published in 1967 by The Brockhampton Press Ltd
Copyright © 1967 Christianna Brand
Illustrations copyright © 1967 Edward Ardizzone

NURSE MATILDA GOES TO HOSPITAL
First published in 1974 by The Brockhampton Press Ltd
Copyright © 1974 Christianna Brand
Illustrations copyright © 1974 Edward Ardizzone

This paperback omnibus edition first published in 2005 by
Bloomsbury Publishing Plc, 36 Soho Square, London W1D 3QY
Text copyright © 1964, 1967, 1974, 2005 Christianna Brand
Illustrations copyright © 1964, 1967, 1974, 2005 Edward Ardizzone
The rights of Christianna Brand and Edward Ardizzone to be identified as the author and
illustrator of this work has been asserted by the Estates of Christianna Brand and Edward
Ardizzone in accordance with the Copyright, Designs and Patents Act, 1988

A CIP catalogue record of this book is available from the British Library
ISBN 0 7475 7899 0

Printed and bound in Great Britain by Clays Ltd, St Ives plc

3

All papers used by Bloomsbury Publishing are natural, recyclable products made from wood
grown in well-managed forests. The manufacturing processes conform to the environmental
regulations of the country of origin.

Contents

NURSE MATILDA

To Tora –
and to our Hilde, with love

Chapter 1

O**NCE** upon a time there was a huge family of children; and they were terribly, terribly naughty.

In those days, mothers and fathers used to have much larger families than they do now; and these large families often *were* naughty. The mothers and fathers had to have all sorts of nurses and nannies and governesses (who were often French or German) to look after all their naughty children: and usually one poor, skinny little nursery-maid to wait on all the nurses and governesses and nannies . . .

This family I'm telling you about seemed to have more children, and naughtier children, than any other. There were so many of them that I shan't even tell you their names but leave you to sort them out as you go along, and add up how many there were. But even their parents had to think of them in groups – there were the Big Ones and the Middling Ones and the Little Ones and the Littlest Ones; and the Baby. The baby was really a splendid character. It had fat, bent legs and its nappy was always falling down round its fat, pink knees; but it kept up with the children to the last ounce of its strength. It talked a curious language all of its own.

There was also the Tiny Baby, but it was so small that it *couldn't* be naughty, so it was very dull and we needn't count it.

The children had two dogs, who were dachshunds. One was a goldeny brown and he was called Brown Sugar or Barley Sugar or sometimes even Demerara Sugar, but anyway, Sugar for short. The other was tiny and black and as sleek as a little seal and she was called Spice.

And the naughtiness of these children was almost past believing. Not a week passed by but the fat nanny or one of the two starchy nurses or the French governess or the skinny little nursery-maid gave notice and had to be replaced by a new fat nanny or starchy nurse or foreign governess or skinny little nursery-maid. Till a day came when they all gave notice together, rising up in a body and marching into the drawing-room and saying with one voice, 'Mr and Mrs Brown' – for that was the name of the children's father and mother – 'your children are so naughty that we can't stand it one minute longer and we're all going away.'

Mrs Brown was very sweet and she never could believe that her children were really naughty. She opened her eyes very wide and said, 'Oh, dear, what have they been doing now?'

So they all began:

'Miss Tora has cut off one of Miss Susie's plaits –'

'– and Master David has made a beard out of it, and glued it on to Miss Charlotte.'

'Master Simon 'ave dress up ze dachshoooond in my best Parees 'at, and take eem for ze promenade.'

'Miss Helen has poured syrup into all the Wellington boots –'

'Miss Stephanie has grated up soap to look like cheese, and now poor Cook's dinner does nothing but foam –'

'– and all the other children are doing simply dreadful things too . . '

'What *you* need,' they added, speaking in

11

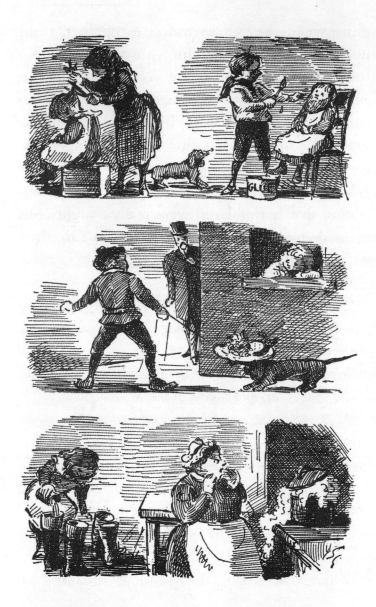

unison, 'is Nurse Matilda.' And they all turned and marched out of the drawing-room and up to their rooms and collected their luggage and got into two cabs and departed.

I'm afraid the children didn't mind a bit. While this had been going on in the drawing-room, they had been busy changing over the contents of the suitcases: and all they could think of was big fat Nanny tomorrow, trying to struggle into the skinny little nursery-maid's dresses; and what the two starchy nurses would look like in Mademoiselle's Paris hats.

'Oh, dear,' sighed Mr and Mrs Brown, 'we shall have to get a new staff of governesses and nurses and nannies.' So they ordered the carriage and drove round to the Agency. The Agency was doubtful, because they had already sent rather a lot of nurses and nannies and governesses to Mr and Mrs Brown's family. 'The person *you* want,' they said, 'is Nurse Matilda.'

'I'm afraid we don't know any Nurse Matilda,' said Mr and Mrs Brown. So the Agency rather reluctantly agreed to send a new nursery staff to the Brown family.

So on Monday a cab drew up at the gate and

out of it poured a new fat nanny and a new governess and two new starchy nurses; and a skinny little nursery-maid, as usual, to wait on them all. Mr and Mrs Brown left the drawing-room and hurried to the front door, all welcoming smiles. But what was their amazement to see nothing but one skinny leg of the nursery-maid disappearing, as she was hauled into the cab – and five horror-stricken faces gazing backwards and upwards as the whole party drove off down the road as fast as it could go. Mr and Mrs Brown rushed out into the drive and looked up, themselves.

At every window of the house (except the drawing-room) stood a group of children, their hair on end, their faces twisted into horrible grimaces, their arms dreadfully waving as they mopped and mowed and lolloped about, obviously in the last stages of the worst kind of lunacy.

'My children!' gasped Mrs Brown. 'My poor, dear, darling children! The dogs have gone mad and bitten them and now they've all gone mad too!'

'Rabies!' cried Mr Brown.

'Hydrophobia!' cried Mrs Brown.

'Raving!' cried Mr Brown.

'Foaming at the mouth!' cried Mrs Brown.

'Only they aren't,' said Mr Brown, calming down a bit and looking up at the children, whose faces were certainly quite innocent of foam; and he looked at the dogs which had rushed out gaily into the garden to speed the departing cab, and added: 'And *they* aren't.' And he grew very thoughtful.

But Mrs Brown was already flying upstairs. She was very sweet, but she was really rather foolish about her poor, dear, darling children. Of course her poor, dear, darling children hadn't been bitten by mad dogs at all, and of course they weren't mad either.

So Mr and Mrs Brown ordered the carriage and drove round to the Agency again.

The Agency was quite cross. 'You simply must get Nurse Matilda,' they said.

'But we don't *know* any Nurse Matilda,' said Mr and Mrs Brown.

'Well – for the very last time,' said the Agency.

'Oh, thank you,' said Mr and Mrs Brown, and they drove hopefully home. At least Mrs Brown

was hopeful. I'm not so sure about Mr Brown.

As it happened, Mr and Mrs Brown had to go out on the following day, so they said to the butler, who was a large, sad, dignified man called Hoppitt, much given to having Feelings in his Bones, 'Hoppitt, if the new nursery staff arrive in the meantime, please give them a nice welcome and take them upstairs to the schoolroom to meet the children.'

'Yes, Sir, yes, Madam,' said Hoppitt, but he thought to himself, Do you call *that* a nice welcome? He had a Feeling in his Bones at this very moment; and it was that Mr and Mrs Brown had been foolish to tell their children how anxious they had been, about their being bitten by mad dogs, and going mad too.

But Mr and Mrs Brown had never thought of that and they drove off, quite untroubled, and on their way back they said to one another, gladly, 'We're earlier than we hoped. Perhaps we'll be in time to meet the new staff, after all.'

Well, they were – in a way. The new staff had just burst out of the front door as Mr and Mrs Brown's carriage drew up to the gate and were streeling down the drive in terrified confusion, led by the governess – she was German, this time – bellowing, '*Hilfe! Hilfe! Die Hunde sind verruckt!*' with a fat nanny waddling frantically in her wake, gasping out, 'Oh, my poor 'eart!' and the two starchy nurses shoving along behind her, hooting, 'Out of our way! Out of our way!' The skinny little nursery-maid dodged between them all, like a boy on a bicycle nipping through the traffic, screeching in a dreadful monotony, 'Ow! Ow! Ow!'

And as they all hurled and tumbled towards the gate, there appeared behind them, to the horror of Mr and Mrs Brown, two small creatures, one brown, one black, their faces covered with a lather of shaving-soap, laced through with tomato ketchup – which ran, barking shrilly and nipping at the heels of the departing staff, while all the children danced in the background crying, 'Run for your lives! Don't let them bite you! They're mad . . .!'

So the next day, Mr and Mrs Brown ordered the carriage, and drove round to the Agency. They didn't wait for the Agency to say anything. They asked at once, 'Can you find Nurse Matilda for us?'

'No, we can't,' said the Agency shortly – for they had heard from the German governess and the nurses and the nanny and the skinny little nursery-maid, as they all streaked through the town on their way to the anti-hydrophobia clinic. And they added firmly: 'And we have Nobody Else On Our Books.'

'Oh, dear!' said Mr and Mrs Brown, and they got into their carriage and drove off to another Agency.

And to another Agency . . .

And to *another* Agency . . .

But it was no good. All the agencies had heard by now all about Mr and Mrs Brown's children and they just shut the door in their faces and peered out through the crack and advised them strongly to get Nurse Matilda.

'If only we could,' sighed poor Mr and Mrs Brown as, at the end of the long day, they took off their hats and coats in the hall.

And as they spoke – lo and behold! – there was a knock at the door, and there stood a small, stout figure dressed in rusty black; and she said, 'Good evening, Mr and Mrs Brown, I am Nurse Matilda.'

Well!

She was very ugly – the ugliest person you ever saw in your life! Her hair was scraped into a bun, sticking straight out at the back of her head like a teapot handle; and her face was very round and wrinkly, and she had eyes like two little black boot-buttons. And her nose! – she had a nose like two potatoes. She wore a rusty black dress right up to the top of her neck and right down to her button boots, and a rusty black jacket and a rusty black bonnet, all trimmed with trembly black jet, with her teapot-handle of a bun sticking out at the back. And she carried a small brown case and a large black stick, and she had a very fierce expression indeed on her wrinkly, round, brown face.

But what you noticed most of all was that she had one huge front Tooth, sticking right out like a tombstone over her lower lip. You never, in the whole of your life, ever saw such a Tooth!

Mrs Brown was quite aghast at the sight of the Tooth. Her poor, dear, darling, blameless angels! She faltered: 'I'm not sure that . . . Well, I mean . . . I don't really know that we need you after all,' and, politely but firmly, she started to close the door.

'Oh, yes, you do,' said Nurse Matilda, and she tapped at the door with her big black stick. Hoppitt usually opened the door – you would hear his dignified footsteps marching unhurriedly towards it – but this time, before he had even appeared from his pantry – suddenly Mr and Mrs Brown found that Nurse Matilda was in the hall with them, and the front door shut after them – if it had ever opened, and they couldn't remember that it had.

'I understand that your children are *exceedingly* naughty,' said Nurse Matilda.

Poor Mrs Brown! 'I don't think . . . I'm quite sure . . . Well, I mean, they're not exactly *naughty* –'

'Yes, they are,' said Mr Brown.

'Mischievous, perhaps. High-spirited. Fun-loving . . .'

'Naughty,' said Mr Brown.

So Mr and Mrs Brown began . . .

'It's true that they won't go to bed –'

'And won't get up –'

'And won't do their lessons –'

'And won't shut doors after them –'

'And won't wear their best clothes –'

'And they do gobble their food –'

'And they will keep running away,' admitted Mrs Brown.

'And they never say "Please" and "Thank you",' added Mr and Mrs Brown together. 'And of course –'

'That will do to go on with,' said Nurse Matilda. 'Your children need me.'

'Well, perhaps,' agreed Mrs Brown doubtfully. 'But,' she added, looking at the Tooth again, 'I don't want to hurt your feelings, but – suppose they don't *want* you?'

'The more they don't want me,' said Nurse Matilda, 'the more they must need me. That is the way I work. When my children don't want me, but do need me: then I must stay. When they no longer need me, but they do want me: then I have to go.' And she smiled at Mr and Mrs Brown, and suddenly it seemed to them that, just for a moment, she wasn't really quite so ugly after all. There was even, Mrs Brown thought, a tear in her bright little boot-button eye. 'It's rather sad,' said Nurse Matilda; 'but there it is!' And she handed her little brown case to Mr Brown to put down by the umbrella-stand in the hall and, still holding her big black stick, started off up the stairs. 'Your children will require seven lessons,' said Nurse Matilda. 'To go to bed when they're told,' she said on the first step. 'Not to gobble,' she said on the second step. 'To do their lessons,' she said on the third step. 'To get up when they're called,' she said on the fourth step. 'To close doors after them, to wear their best clothes when they have to; and not to run away,' she said on the fifth, sixth and seventh steps. ' "Please" – and – "Thank – you" – will – look – after – them – selves,' she added on the remaining nine steps up to the turn of the stairs, one word to a step; and she turned and looked down at Mr and Mrs Brown, standing helpless, gazing back at her from the hall. 'Don't trouble about me. I shall find my own way,' said Nurse Matilda and stumped on up to the first floor, where the schoolroom was.

Chapter 2

HEN Nurse Matilda opened the schoolroom door, the children had finished their supper and were waiting for bedtime – though of course they had no intention of going to bed. And this is what they were doing:

Francesca had filled the Tiny Baby's bottle with baby-food and was feeding the dogs with it.

Little Quentin had drawn flowers all up the walls and was watering them from the big, brown, nursery teapot.

Antony was filling up the nursery ink-wells with runny red jam.

Nicolas had collected all the Little Ones' dolls and was lining them up for execution.

Sophie was shampooing Henrietta's hair with glue.

All the other children were doing simply dreadful things too.

When Nurse Matilda came in, they all went straight on with what they were doing.

'Good evening, children,' said Nurse Matilda, and she gave a loud thump on the floor with her big black stick. 'I am Nurse Matilda.'

Nobody took the faintest notice; but Christianna gave a large wink at the rest of them and said, 'How funny! The door's opened, but nobody has come in.'

They all knew quite well that the door had opened and Nurse Matilda had come in.'

'And now it's closed again,' said Caro, 'and still nobody has come in.'

'*I* have come in,' said Nurse Matilda. 'I am Nurse Matilda.'

'Did anyone speak?' said Jaci, pretending to seem surprised.

'*I* didn't hear anything,' said Almond.

'*I* didn't hear anyfink,' said Little Sarah.

'Go gear, go gear!' cried the Baby, joyfully. This was the language the Baby spoke – all of its own.

'Well, all listen carefully,' said Nurse Matilda, 'and try to hear this. You are to stop what you're doing and put all your things away and go to bed.'

Everybody went straight on with what he was doing. Francesca went on feeding the dachshunds, Quentin went on watering the nursery walls, Antony went on pouring jam into the ink-wells . . .

Nurse Matilda looked them all over quietly with her black, beady eyes; and then she thumped once more on the floor with her stick.

After a while, the jam ran out over the top of the ink-well and all over Antony's hands. He licked it off, but he still went on pouring, the jam still went on running over, and he had to lick and lick and soon he felt quite sick. This is silly, he thought. All I've got to do is to stop pouring jam into the ink-well! But he couldn't stop: try as he would, he couldn't stop pouring jam into the ink-well and so the jam went on running and he went on licking, and soon he was feeling a very ill boy indeed. He cast a despairing look at Nicolas.

Nicolas had executed all the dolls – they lay in a long row, headless, and now he seemed to be casting round for more victims, teddy bears, golliwogs, stuffed animals of every kind. The Little Ones, stricken to their hearts by this massacre of their treasures, were howling dismally,

clinging to his legs and arms, pulling his hair half out, in their anxiety – and yet he went on collecting, went on lining the poor creatures up and, whack, whack, whack, lopping off their sad heads. Even his own precious army of tin soldiers was now in a neat row, stolidly waiting to die.

And Francesca was stuffing baby-food down the dogs' throats, stuff, stuff, stodge, stodge, and the dogs were full up with baby-food right to the top, and they didn't like it any more and were fearsomely growling. Francesca looked scared –

she had never known Sugar and Spice to growl before; and *they* were looking surprised because they never did growl; but still she went on feverishly mixing baby-food and every time they opened their mouths to give another growl, she poked more food down them.

And Quentin went on pouring and pouring tea down the walls and the teapot seemed quite inexhaustible. The floor was two inches deep in tea, and their feet were all wet; and everyone who wasn't executing dolls or feeding dogs or licking jam or shampooing hair – by this time Sophie and Hetty were stuck together like Siamese twins, struggling stickily to get apart, but Sophie still went on pouring glue over Hetty's head, both of them weeping with rage and resentment – by this time, everyone who wasn't otherwise employed, was stamping about with soaking wet feet, quite brown with tea water, telling Quentin to stop it. But Quentin wouldn't stop it. The fact was that he *couldn't* stop it. Any more than Francesca or Antony or Nicolas or Sophie could stop it . . .

And by now all they longed to do was to stop it and go to bed. But you see, they couldn't.

Well, they didn't like giving in. But at last they did say, crossly and grudgingly: 'Oh, do let's stop this and go to bed.'

'Say "Please",' said Nurse Matilda.

'We never say "Please",' said the children.

'Well, then, you'll never get to bed,' said Nurse Matilda.

'Oh, all right – "Please", then,' said the children.

'Peag, geng,' said the Baby, in its own language.

And Nurse Matilda looked at them and she smiled a little smile: and – it was very odd, but just for a moment her fierce round face with its boot-button eyes and its nose like two potatoes, didn't look quite so fierce after all: and except for the Tooth, not even quite so ugly.

And she gave one sharp rap with her stick on the floor – and all of a sudden, the floor began to dry up and all the tea began to run glop, glop, glop, *backwards*, into the teapot. And all the tins of baby-food were empty, which they hadn't been up to that minute, and the bottle stopped pouring itself into the dogs and they gave themselves a great shake, no growls any more, and ran off quite hungrily to have their own dinners from the bowls in the nursery corner. And Nicolas stopped executing dolls and their heads flew back again, ping, ping, ping, on to their necks. And Sophie and Hetty came apart with a terrific squelch and the glue ran in a little river towards the dolls and got between their heads and their necks and stuck their heads back on again . . .

And Nurse Matilda gave another sharp rap with her stick; and in that one second, it seemed to the children, every child was sitting in its nice, warm, cosy bed, all clean and neat, hands scrubbed, face washed, teeth brushed, hair combed, prayers said – with no idea in the world as to how it got there.

Nurse Matilda went quietly downstairs and reported to Mr and Mrs Brown: 'Lesson One,' she said.

Chapter 3

BEFORE breakfast next morning, Nurse Matilda sent the children out to the garden for some Healthful Fresh Air. When she called them in again, this is what they were doing:

David had cut all the gardener's best marrows and put them into the pigsty; and the old sow was at her wit's end, because she thought she had suddenly got eight brand-new babies to look after. Stephanie had made herself a nose out of two potatoes and was pretending to be Nurse Matilda. Toni had persuaded the Little Ones that they were really ducks and they were sitting in the muddy grass round the pond, earnestly trying to lay eggs.

And the Baby had toddled down to the front gate and was pleading, 'Alms for ge lovey Aggy!' and holding out the little nursery potty to passers by. All the other children were doing simply dreadful things too.

Nurse Matilda appeared at the breakfast-room window and rang a large bell. No one took any notice. David added a ninth marrow to the family of the distracted old sow. Stephanie banged about with a large stick (but I must admit, she did it with her face turned away from the real Nurse Matilda); Toni urged on the Little-ies in their egg-laying efforts. And then, suddenly . . . A funny sort of feeling began to creep over the children . . . Supposing that, once again, it wasn't so much that they *wouldn't* stop, as that they *couldn't* stop!

They all stopped rather quickly, while they still could: and went in to breakfast.

After a little while Nurse Matilda said: 'There is no need to gobble.'

But they did gobble. They always gobbled. They liked breakfast. They liked their porridge so stiff that it would spin round in its own milk like a little island. They liked to write their names, each on his own island of porridge, with a thin thread of treacle dripping from the spoon. And they liked their boiled eggs, and turned them upside down in the egg-cups when they'd finished, to look like whole new eggs; and they liked their mugs of milk or tea, and their lovely fresh home-made bread and butter. So they went on gobbling: snatching bread and butter from under one another's noses, scooping out the last of the jam without caring who else wanted it, holding out their mugs for more, without a 'Please' or 'Thank you' . . .

Nurse Matilda sat at the top of the table, her big black stick in her hand.

Down went the porridge, down went the eggs, down went the bread and butter and jam.

And more bread and butter and jam.

And *more* bread and butter and jam.

And *more* bread and butter and jam and *more* bread and butter and jam and MORE and MORE and MORE bread and butter and jam . . .

'Here,' said the children with their mouths full, 'that's enough!' only their mouths were so full that what they said sounded like 'Assawuff,' and Nurse Matilda only looked politely puzzled and said, 'Did you ask for more porridge?' and to every child's utter horror, there before it was a

plate of porridge all over again, spinning dizzily with its golden signature in its sea of milk. And their hands seized up their spoons and down went the porridge, stuff, stuff, stodge, stodge, on top of all that bread and butter. And suddenly all those upside-down eggshells really *were* full, new eggs; and up and down flashed their egg-spoons choking down egg on top of porridge; and on top of the egg came more and more of that dreadful bread and butter and jam . . . And then the porridge started all over again . . .

The children puffed and blew, their cheeks

bulged, their eyes goggled. They felt that at any moment they would blow up and burst. They longed to cry out for mercy. They would even have said 'Please' if they had thought of it. They would have done anything if only they could have stopped eating. But they couldn't; until at last they suddenly had a brilliant idea. The next time the porridge came round, they forced and fought with their own right hands until the hands just managed to write, with treacle, on the islands of porridge, 'STOP!'

Nurse Matilda looked at the plates of porridge. 'Say "Please",' she said.

They had to wait all through the eggs and the bread and butter till porridge came round again; and then write 'PLEASE!'

And Nurse Matilda smiled. (And really, was she quite so ugly as they had thought her last night?)

And she banged with her big black stick on the floor; and suddenly all the children were standing up quietly behind their chairs and saying their grace.

Nurse Matilda joined Mr and Mrs Brown, who were having their own breakfast in the dining-room. 'Lesson Two,' she said.

Chapter 4

WHEN Nurse Matilda went up to the schoolroom to begin the first morning's lessons, the children were sitting all round the huge table as good as gold. She sat down and looked round at them steadily. She said: 'Why are Sophie and Hetty wearing their hats?'

'They can't get used to having short hair,' said Simon. 'They're shy of showing their long ears.' And he added: 'It's very awkward, but they seem to have turned into dachshunds.'

'And we've turned into children,' said two very growly voices from under the table.

Nurse Matilda lifted a corner of the red, bobble-edged schoolroom tablecloth, and there, curled up on the floor, were the dachshunds; which, however, certainly did look very much like two little girls in brown Holland pinafores.

And she looked beneath the brims of the round, grey felt hats, and saw two long, goldeny jowls, and two black, moist noses, and two pairs of bright, slightly bewildered eyes. And she gave a little tap with her stick and at once there came from under the table two short, sharp barks and she said: 'Oh, dear, I think the dogs need to be let out,' and bent down and took them by the scruffs of their pinafores and led them to the door and down the stairs and into the garden: and pushed them outside and closed the garden door on them. And try as they might to say, 'We're only pretending, we're not really dachsies at all, we're really Sophie and Hetty,' all they could do was to utter piteous growls and whines.

Nurse Matilda went back to the schoolroom. She said: 'We will begin with arithmetic.'

'Umps rumps,' said all the children, readily.

'What do you mean?' said Nurse Matilda.

'Oh, don't you know?' said Tora. 'That's Fuddledutch. We once had a Fuddledutch governess and I'm afraid we can't do arithmetic in anything else.' She repeated it in Fuddledutch (a language known only to the Brown children). 'We wumps humps a Fuddledumps gumpsmumps

and we cumps dumps Arumpsmatumps in
anythumps umps.'

'I see,' said Nurse Matilda: and she turned a
page and asked in perfect Fuddledutch (only far
faster than any of them could speak it): 'Well,
then, humps mumps is thumpety thrumps
divumps bumps numps?'

Roger tried to say, 'Seventy-three divided by
nine goes eight and three over,' but he couldn't.
He found himself answering, 'Umps and thrumps
umps.'

'Wrong,' said Nurse Matilda and she turned to the golden-brown faces beneath the round felt hats.

'Eight and one over,' said two rather barky voices in unison; and two pairs of bright, little, twinkly eyes looked out from beneath the hat brims with kindly pity.

'Right. But the rest of you had better all learn your tables. Now then: Twice one are two . . .' said Nurse Matilda. She added, sharply: 'Sit up!'

The children continued to lounge in their chairs, and they said not a word – not even, 'Twumps wumps are twumps.' But already they were doubtful. Already, deep within them, little voices were saying, 'Are you quite wise . . .?' And, sure enough, even as they lounged there, the backs of the chairs – those dear old familiar schoolroom chairs, where they had lounged through their lessons with all their poor, harassed governesses up to now – seemed very hard and high; and the backs poked into *their* backs, and the seats had little splinters which stuck into *their* seats, if they wriggled; and if they tipped backwards only just the littlest bit, the whole chair went over with a crash and landed them on the floor with their legs in the air – and there

they stuck! By the time the morning break came, every one of them was sitting up straight except those who were lying on their backs, looking silly, with their legs in the air.

When the time came for cocoa and biscuits at eleven, Nurse Matilda took hers with Mr and Mrs Brown in Mrs Brown's little boudoir.

'How are the children progressing?' said Mr Brown.

'I think we have mastered Lesson Three,' said Nurse Matilda, smiling; and after she had gone back to the schoolroom, Mrs Brown said to Mr Brown, 'Do you know, when she smiles she really looks almost pretty. Except, of course,' she added, 'for that terrible Tooth.'

Chapter 5

NEXT morning the children wouldn't get up.

Some days it was like that – they just *wouldn't* get up. The nurses and governesses used to beg them and plead with them, and get them by the arms and tug at them, but they wouldn't get up. If at last some of them were bodily pulled out of bed, then they waited till the grown-ups turned their attention to some of the others, and by the time the poor exhausted nurses looked round, the first lot had hopped back into bed and humped the blankets over their heads and were making dreadful noises, pretending to snore. Once they all got into bed upside-down, and the nurses got awful shocks because when they angrily pulled back the bed-clothes and said, 'Get up!' there were two feet asleep on the pillow. And once they all swopped beds with each other, and Nanny nearly had a fit, because when she went to get the Baby from the cot it was making the most peculiar noises, and she thought *it* was having a fit, but it was really huge Simon curled up, nearly bulging the sides of the cot out, and the noise was him, trying to stop laughing. And once they all put dummies in their beds and got under the beds, and Nanny and the nurses and the governess all got more shocks; though perhaps that wasn't exactly not getting up. But, anyway, on this morning, they wouldn't.

Nurse Matilda stood in the doorway and now I'm afraid she didn't look pretty at all; and not a bit smiley, either – short and squat, she looked, like an angry old toad, in her rusty black dress, with her hair done up at the back in its teapot handle and her little dark eyes all glittery and her great big Tooth, and her nose like two potatoes; holding her big black stick. She said for the second time: 'Get up!'

Everybody snored dreadfully. Nobody moved.

Nurse Matilda lifted her big black stick and suddenly all the snores stopped. Eyes opened and peeped out from beneath the humps of blankets. They couldn't help remembering those other times when Nurse Matilda had banged with her stick.

Nurse Matilda noted the silence and the bright eyes peeping and she lowered her stick. 'I shall give you half an hour,' she said, 'to be up and dressed and washed, teeth cleaned, pyjamas folded, windows opened, beds turned back; and out into the garden for some Healthful Fresh Air before breakfast. The Big Ones will look after the Little Ones.' And she went away.

Well!

They were out of bed in two seconds after her back was turned – but not to wash and dress. They had never given way before and they weren't going to now. On the other hand – that stick! There was a great scuttering between the boys' rooms and the girls' rooms, to confer; a great deal of whispering and planning; a great flurry of activity – a wild scampering back to bed when Nurse Matilda's footfall was heard once more. When Nurse Matilda said, 'Why haven't you got up?' they all said: 'We can't get up. We're ill.'

'Ill?' said Nurse Matilda. (And it *was* very sudden.)

'We've got codes id our dozes,' said Roger.

'Ad paids id our piddies,' said Tora.

'Ad spots,' said Louisa.

'Ad tebratures,' said Simon.

'Ad we feel sick,' said Fenella.

'We thig id bust be the beasles,' said Teresa.

'All gock meagig,' said the Baby in its own language.

And, sure enough, when Nurse Matilda looked, she saw that their faces were as white as clowns', and covered with huge red (paint-box) spots.

'Very well,' said Nurse Matilda; and she banged once with her stick and went away. The children started immediately to scramble out of bed. But . . . Yes – you've guessed! They couldn't. They just had to stay there, humped under the blankets – which were suddenly dreadfully hot and scratchy

– and their noses felt dreadfully stuffy and they had pains in their pinnies and weren't at all sure that they weren't really going to be sick. And they put up their languid hands to their hot faces and tried to wipe away the spots – and the spots wouldn't go. And the dreadful truth dawned upon them at last: *they really had got measles.*

Poor Mrs Brown was in a terrible state when she learned that all her children had got measles.

'Leave it to me,' said Nurse Matilda calmly. 'I quite understand the disease.' And she laid down her rules. No noise. No light. Nothing to eat or drink. And of course – *no getting out of bed.*

Mrs Brown was horrified. Her poor, darling children! 'Nothing to eat?'

'Not while they have these pains.'

'And nothing to drink?'

'Not while they feel so sick.'

'No noise? Not even talking –?'

'Not while their colds are so bad that they talk through their noses.'

'And no light? Can't they even look at books?'

'Not while they have such high temperatures!' said Nurse Matilda, quite shocked. She added: 'However, of course there will be Doses.' And she produced three huge bottles of medicine and ranged them side by side on the mantelpiece: a black bottle and a red bottle and a dreadful yellowy-green bottle.

'For the fever,' said Nurse Matilda, going round with the black bottle.

'For the pains,' she said, going round with the red bottle.

'For the spots,' she said, going round with the yellowy-green bottle.

The yellowy-green one was the worst; but, all in all they were three of the nastiest medicines the Brown children had ever had to take in all their lives. They had a large tablespoon of each of them, every single hour.

'*Hog*ging meggikig,' said the Baby.

'No talking,' said Nurse Matilda – even to the Baby.

It was a long, long day. To Mr and Mrs Brown, it seemed like ten days, which is the time that measles usually lasts; and I can assure you it seemed like ten days to the children too. There they lay, huddled up under the hot, prickly blankets, and their heads ached and their tummies ached and they felt sick, and when they raised their poor, dull heads to look at the others, the others looked awful, all covered with enormous spots. And of course as the hours passed by and the pains got better and they didn't feel so sick, they began to get dreadfully hungry. And only then did they remember that it was Wednesday and that Wednesday was their favourite-dinner day. On Wednesday there was steak-and-kidney pudding, the crust dry and light on top and all sloshy and gooey underneath as it ought to be, wallowing in its hot, rich gravy; and mashed potatoes with a little cheese in them to make them all goldeny, and swedes, not boiled in water at all, but sliced up thin and cooked in nothing but butter (speciality of Cook). And treacle roly-poly, just as they loved it – not a solid bolster of pudding with some syrup poured over it, but a thin layer rolled out and spread with great dollops of treacle and then rolled up again lightly; so that every inch of it was simply oozy with gold . . .

I know it was a dreadfully indigestible meal, but Mrs Brown always gave her children whatever they liked best, every single day of the week.

But there was no steak-and-kidney, or treacle roll today. Instead, beneath their windows they

heard the tramp of feet and clatter of dishes and the voices of Hoppitt and Cook upon a melancholy mission. Hoppitt had placed a large table outside the gate, with a notice saying, SPARE STEAK-AND-KIDNEY PUDS, MASHED POTATOES, SWEDES (SPECIALITY OF COOK) AND TREACLE ROLY-POLIES FOR ANYONE WHO WANTS THEM. GOING WASTE ON ACCOUNT OF MEASLES. NO CHARGE, BUT PLEASE PUT ANYTHING YOU WISH TO DONATE INTO MONEY-BOX SUPPLIED.

I'm afraid the money-box supplied had been supplied by Hoppitt and Cook; but still it had been their idea in the first place.

So there the children lay and longed for steak-and-kidney pudding and treacle roly-poly and thought with rage and gloom that the village children would be having the time of their lives. They waged continual war with the village children, who were led by a huge and terrible boy called Podge. He will be podgier than ever after this, thought the Brown children, resentfully.

But they must lie and suffer; and now that their headaches were going, they'd have liked to look at books, but the curtains were drawn and even if they could have seen to read, they weren't allowed to; and as for talking, every time they opened their mouths, Nurse Matilda was there with a large spoonful of medicine. By the time dusk fell and she came to tuck them up – she had to begin early, there were so many of them – and give them their final doses (double this time, 'To last them through the night'), the children were ready to say humbly, 'Tomorrow morning – can we get up?'

'Can you what?' said Nurse Matilda.

'Can we get up?'

'Can you what?' said Nurse Matilda.

'Cay peag,' said the Baby.

'Oh, yes: can we get up, *please*?' said the children.

And Nurse Matilda smiled and she gave a little

tap with her stick and she went away; and when she had gone the children never even mentioned the Tooth. They just said to one another, 'Just for a moment – didn't she look *pretty*?'

Next morning, when Nurse Matilda came to the door, the children were up and washed and dressed and had cleaned their teeth and folded their pyjamas and opened the windows and turned back their beds and were ready to go down to the garden for some Healthful Fresh Air before breakfast. The Big Ones were leading the Little Ones by the hand. Nurse Matilda said nothing; but she asked Hoppitt to take a message to Mr and Mrs Brown with their breakfast.

'Nurse's compliments, Madam,' said Hoppitt, 'and I am to say "Lesson Four".'

'Oh, thank you, Hoppitt,' said Mrs Brown. 'And do you know if the children are better?'

'That I don't know, Madam,' said Hoppitt. 'But I have – if you will pardon the expression, Sir and Madam – a Feeling in my Bones that they are going to be.' And he added, in a very rare burst of confidence: 'Nurse Matilda herself is *looking* – well, better, this morning.'

Chapter 6

OU needn't think that from then on the Brown children were always good – indeed they weren't! They were naughty the very next day, as you're going to see. I suppose they were so much in the habit of it, that they couldn't get used to being good; and, anyway, they had only come to Lesson Four.

But just for that day, they *were* good; and they had to confess, even when they got naughty again, that they had had a wonderful time.

It was a lovely day and Nurse Matilda gave them their lessons in the garden. But such lessons! First they had history, and the lawn was the Atlantic Ocean, and the shrubbery on the other side of it was America, and they got out the old pony trap – fetched from the coachhouse – and that was the *Mayflower*; and they all piled in and sailed across the Atlantic, being frightfully seasick over the sides of the pony trap and constantly crying out, 'Land ahoy!' and being dreadfully disappointed when it wasn't. By the mid-morning break for milk and biscuits, even the Baby could say 'Game-ge-gurk,' and 'Kickgeen-hungigan-kenki', and 'Ge Gaykower,' which as Nurse Matilda seemed to know, quite without the children translating for her, meant James the First and sixteen hundred and twenty and the *Mayflower*. As *you* know, of course, that was when the *Mayflower* sailed.

And after the break they had French, and half the children were verbs and the other half were verb-endings, and they played a new kind of hide-and-seek, finding their own endings; and then it was time for lunch.

'This afternoon,' said Nurse Matilda when lunch was over, 'we will go for a walk – and do arithmetic.'

'Oh, lor'!' said the children, losing heart. (Fancy a *walk*! And *arithmetic*!)

But Nurse Matilda's arithmetic was very different from the governesses' arithmetic. Nurse Matilda made them pretend that they had only so many arms and legs between them, not enough to go round. Some of them had to hop and some of them, who had no legs at all, had to be carried (fortunately these were mostly the smaller ones), and the armless ones had to walk along looking very stiff and stout with their coats buttoned right over their real arms, which were pinned down to their bodies by the buttoned-up coats, and their sleeves hanging empty. So then they began to re-divide the arms and legs, to try and even things out; and in this way the Little Ones learnt adding and taking away – 'take away one leg from Justin, who has two, and give it to poor Dominic, who has none. Arabella and Joanna and Susannah have four arms between them; give them one each, and that'll be three and one over . . .' And the Bigger Ones learnt money sums by making prices for an arm or a leg; and those who had too few, bargained with those who had enough – or, as soon happened if you were good at bargaining, too many.

Tora, who was terribly bad at arithmetic, ended up just a sort of pillow, poor thing, with – officially – no arms and legs at all; while Antony, who was always very good at money – perhaps because when he was little he had swallowed a penny and become rather a hero with his brothers and sisters – had four arms and three legs and somehow managed to be one and tuppence richer as well. However, he was a very kind boy and he went back and sold Tora a leg for her last tuppence, so at least she was able to hop; and he held her up, because of course, having no arms, she couldn't hang on to him. Otherwise, as she was one of the Big Ones – too big to be carried – she'd have had to stay planted by the wayside, till they picked her up on the way back and lent her a leg, just to get home with.

That night, when Nurse Matilda saw them all into bed, she really did – except for the Tooth – look all smiles and almost beautiful. The children thought they would never, never, never be naughty again.

But next morning when they woke up, you won't be surprised to hear they were just as naughty as ever.

When Nurse Matilda sent them to get some Healthful Fresh Air before breakfast, they didn't go out at all. They said to one another, 'Let's go through the Baize Door.'

In those days, when there were such big families, they needed lots of people to look after them, and the houses were divided into two parts: very often by a door covered with baize – green or red – and studded with big, round brass nails. On one side of the Baize Door lived the Family, and on the other side lived the Staff. In the Browns' case, the Staff was Hoppitt and Cook; and Celeste, the French lady's maid, who looked after Mrs Brown; and Ellen, the parlourmaid, and Alice-and-Emily, the housemaids, who were always thought of like that, linked together like Siamese twins; and Evangeline, the 'tweeny'. Poor Evangeline, she was dreadfully put upon by the rest; but she was a cheerful little lump and I don't think she really minded.

Children – especially the Browns – were strictly forbidden ever to go through the Baize Door unless they were specially invited by the Staff. I must confess that the Brown children were very seldom invited.

But that morning – worn out by goodness, I suppose; they certainly weren't used to it – the children did go through the Baize Door; and what's more they didn't close it. You remember that one of the things Mr and Mrs Brown had told Nurse Matilda was that the children never could be got to close doors after themselves. 'Remember the Door!' their parents would cry out frantically. But the children never did. And they didn't close the Baize Door this morning, either.

Hoppitt and Cook and Celeste and Ellen and Alice-and-Emily were all having breakfast in the Staff Room (waited on by Evangeline) before the family breakfast was served. When they came back to the kitchen, this is what the children were doing:

Sophie had taken Hoppitt's grey woollen socks from the airer and was stirring them into the porridge.

Hetty had made a stiff paste of flour and water and was putting it through the mangle.

Justin had covered the seat of Cook's chair with dripping.

Almond had found Celeste's powder and paint and was giving the raw breakfast sausages dear little faces.

Agatha was giving the dogs a bath in the stock-pot.

And all the other children were doing simply dreadful things too.

The children took one look at Hoppitt and

Cook and Celeste and Ellen and Alice-and-Emily, and ran out through the Baize Door as fast as they could, and shut it tight after them, and leant against it. On the other side, they could hear a fearful roaring and clucking and ooh-la-la-ing as Hoppitt and Cook and Celeste and Ellen and Alice-and-Emily found out what had happened to the socks and the mangle and the chair and the sausages and the stock-pot.

I'm afraid there was also a loud tee-hee-hee-ing; which, however, stopped abruptly as a commanding voice cried: 'Evangeline! – Get that door open!'

The children held on to the door with all their might. 'She can't!' they called back. 'We're safe!'

Nurse Matilda stood on the stairs above them, looking down; and she lifted her big black stick. . .

And the door swung suddenly inwards and all the children rumbled into the kitchen on top of one another, in a heap of arms and legs and heads and shoulders, and conveniently up-turned behinds.

Hoppitt and Cook, without a word, handed to Evangeline a large, flat frying-pan.

Whack, whack, whack, went the frying- pan.

The children howled and struggled and fought and at last were all on their feet again and back on the other side of the door. But hold that door as they might — it wouldn't close. It was very strange: all those children! – and they couldn't get a door to close.

And as it swung to and fro, they could see into the kitchen where Cook and Hoppitt and Celeste and Ellen and Alice-and-Emily were arming Evangeline for total war. She advanced at last, urged forward by willing arms and conjurations to Be Brave! On her head was a huge black enamel saucepan, down her stout front hung a big roasting dish, in one hand she carried the frying-pan (somewhat dented now) and in the other, Cook's rolling-pin. On her large, round face was a look of great unwillingness and doubt; but behind her was Hoppitt with the carving fork, prodding her on.

The children began to back away through the hall to the front door. Cries of 'Open the door!' 'Make for the garden!' rent the air. 'Go in ge gargy! Oping ge gor!' cried the Baby, backing away as fast as its short, fat legs would carry it. As usual, its nappy seemed just about to fall down.

But, just as the other door wouldn't shut – the front door wouldn't open. They pulled and they tugged, they struggled with the lock, they rattled the big bolts, they swung on the chain, but nothing would open the door. And advancing upon them, armoured in tin, Evangeline approached with uplifted frying-pan. But . . .

'After all,' said Daniel, suddenly. 'It's only Evangeline.'

All the children stopped struggling with the door and stared. The door immediately flew open, but they took no notice of it.

'After all,' they said. 'It's only Evangeline.'

'Ongy Egangykeeng,' said the Baby.

Nurse Matilda looked down from the stairs. She looked at the faces of the children, all smiles of relief, and she looked at Evangeline's large, round, unwilling face; and she thumped once more with her stick. And in that very instant, out of the kitchen, helmeted in sauce-pans, hung about with baking-tins, armed with frying-pans and rolling-pins and brooms and mops and flat-irons and a huge pair of curling tongs (Celeste!) dashed Hoppitt and Cook and Celeste and Ellen and Alice-and-Emily; and brushed Evangeline aside and came on . . .

The children were out of that open door before it had time to close on them again, and into the garden.

The kitchen army gave chase. Down the drive . . . Across the wide lawn . . . Out of the shrubbery, into the high-walled kitchen garden; scrambling through netting, between tall bean-rows, dodging among raspberry canes . . . The Little Ones got lost in a forest of blackcurrant bushes, the Middling Ones tripped over marrow trailers and had to be gone back for and hoicked up and set running again; squashed tomato, overripe gooseberry exploded and skidded beneath their pounding feet. The Baby's nappy had come down and was right round its ankles.

Into the greenhouse – door wouldn't shut after them to keep the pursuers back; out through a window to a crash of breaking glass and the rage of the gardener . . . Over the wall, down the gravelled paths, leaping flowerbeds, tearing through rose-bushes, running, running, running . . .

Running so fast that before they even thought of the pond, they were teetering on the grassy bank – skidding – tippling – and at last, splish splosh! splish splosh! were head-long into the middle of it, up to their waists in water and mud.

Hoppitt and Cook and Celeste and Ellen and

Alice-and-Emily and Evangeline got to the bank and, with frantically flailing arms to keep their balance, came to a halt and stood glaring. The children moved into the middle of the pond and defiantly glared back.

Hoppitt, of course, had established himself as generalissimo. He made a commanding gesture. 'Come out!' he cried, and added an expression that Evangeline knew only too well. 'And do it smartish!'

'No,' said Lindy; and threw a lump of pond mud at him.

Well!

The mud took Hoppitt, bonk! on the middle

of his nose. But his dignity never wavered.

'Very well,' he said. 'You've asked for it.'

And now the children saw that, through thick and thin, he had carried with him the porridge saucepan.

The pond was very large and shallow and also very muddy. The children, clustering together in the very centre of it, stood their ground – if you could call it ground when it was actually such very soft, gooey, oozy, chocolatey, brown-black mud. Cook and Celeste and Ellen and Alice-and-Emily and Evangeline fanned out and made a circle round the edge of it. There was no escape; and now Hoppitt was seen to be passing among his troops, handing out porridge-soaked socks.

The battle was on.

Fortunately, only Hoppitt was a very good aim. The children recovered the floating socks and returned them, with a little good, black mud added for interest. *Their* aim was much better and soon the faces round the pond were a curious lumpy grey, streaked with black: only the eyes stared out balefully from beneath the kitchen saucepans. The socks flew back and forth, but by now they were losing their splendid coatings of porridge. Hoppitt dipped them back into the saucepan and reissued them. The children used the interval to wash their own faces in the pond. The effect was somewhat stripy, and bindweed tangled itself over them and hung down about their ears, like green hair; but at least they didn't have to keep licking-in porridge. The staff on the bank couldn't wash, and beneath the cold oatmeal, their poor faces were growing very stiff.

When the porridge was exhausted, Cook produced the dough from the mangle.

The children were beginning to get rather desperate. All they had to fight back with was mud; and now Alice-and-Emily had armed themselves with mops and brooms, and every time a child stooped to scoop up more mud, it found itself held under with a large kitchen mop. Fortunately, the Littlest Ones, who might have been a difficulty, were simply loving it. With all those nannies and nurses and governesses, they had very seldom had a chance to play in really dirty water. (I think Nurse Matilda, when she banged with her stick, always saw that the Little Ones didn't suffer too badly.)

But even to entertain the Little Ones, you

couldn't stand throwing mud and dough for ever: especially as, now that the dough was finished, Hoppitt could simply send Evangeline to the kitchen for fresh ammunition.

'Bring them sausages that they drew faces on,' he commanded.

'And all them jellies and blancmanges,' added Cook, 'that I set aside for nursery tea.'

The children took counsel among themselves.

'What we want is a hostage!'

'A gockig, a gockig!' cried the Baby, splashing up and down in the mud, looking like a chocolate baby, made to be eaten.

'I'll get Cook,' said Sally, at once.

Cook was laughing. She was standing at the edge of the pond with Hoppitt, and she was laughing at the thought of the children seeing all their lovely jellies and blancmanges used as ammunition. But the children really hated jelly and blancmange and had only ever pretended to eat them, so as not to hurt Cook's feelings. It did seem ungrateful of her to be laughing – and, anyway, so unlike Cook to be unkind. But everything was – well, *strange* – today.

Cook was laughing so much that she never

even noticed Sally, slithering up out of the mud like an otter, and tying her stout ankles together with a piece of bindweed. When Evangeline returned, tacking across the lawn towards them, quite blinded by her high load of jellies and blancmanges, with the sausages coiled on top, Cook reached out and took the sausages, and threw one end straight at the huddle of children in the pond: and kicked her legs up in the air with joy.

But instead of her legs going two ways, as she intended – being tied together, they both went the same way; and Cook sat down upon her broad sit-upon, with a bump that shook the banks of the pond and set the jellies and blancmanges all a-wobble; and, well greased with the dripping that the children had put on her

chair — she began to slide down the grassy slope towards the water. And the children seized one end of the chain of sausages and tugged: and in her bewilderment, Cook quite forgot to let go of the other end.

It was a pretty desperate situation, all round. On the bank, Hoppitt and Ellen had got hold of Cook by the ears — her hair was not her own, so there was no use hanging on to that — and were holding on for dear life, to prevent her being taken hostage. In the pond, the children hauled on the line of sausages and drew her slowly down.

But the bottom of the pond was soft and slithery, and gradually their weight, as they hauled, was driving them deeper and deeper down into it — down to their ankles, down to their knees — the Little Ones were in it up to their waists . . . Yet they dared not let go or they would lose their hostage; and then here they would be, stuck fast in the mud, a helpless prey to onslaughts of jelly and blancmange; not to mention the brooms and mops and even the rolling-pin and the flat-iron and Celeste's curling tongs. What nips Celeste would give them with those curling tongs when she remembered her lost powder and paint, all lavished on those little smiling sausage faces . . .!

And meanwhile the mud was almost up to their necks. Oh dear, thought the children, if only we hadn't gone through the Baize Door! If only we could have got it to shut! For that matter, they couldn't help ruefully adding, if only we *ever* shut doors!

And as they said it, the Baby cried gleefully (large bubbles of mud coming out of its mouth, it being so much shorter than the others and nearly submerged by now), 'Gairg Nurk Magiggy!'

And there she was indeed: standing quietly on the lawn, watching them – though they felt quite sure she hadn't been there before.

'Oh, Nurse Matilda,' they all cried out, 'do help us!'

'Cay peag,' said the Baby; but almost before it had said it – this time, they all added: 'Please!'

And Nurse Matilda smiled; and as she smiled, suddenly all sorts of things began to happen. As Hoppitt and Ellen hauled, and the children hauled, with the line of smiling sausages stretched out taut between them, a small *brown* shape flew

through the water and a set of sharp little white teeth bit through the chain of sausages. And at the same time, a little *black* shape flew up the bank and, with another set of white teeth, snapped up Cook's hair from between Hoppitt's and Ellen's hands and fled off across the lawn with it. And Hoppitt and Ellen were so astonished to find Cook with a bald pink head on top of her round, mud-black face, that they let go of her ears and she slid right down off the bank and into the arms of the enemy. At the same time, with great suckings and squelchings, the children's feet came suddenly out of the mud.

They were free! They had their hostage, the enemy was staring, helpless, from the bank. All they needed was some ammunition of their own, and the day was theirs.

'Oh, Nurse Matilda,' they prayed in their hearts. 'Please! *Please!*'

And Nurse Matilda smiled again; and Evangeline, whose pile of jellies and blanc-manges was still too high for the poor thing to see where she was going – eager all this time to find out what on earth was happening all about her – walked slap into the pond, tripped over some bindweed, tipped slowly forward and deposited her load bang in front of the children . . .

Hoppitt and Celeste and Ellen and Alice-and-Emily took one look at poor Cook, quite bald and covered with chocolate-coloured mud; and at Evangeline standing with her empty tray, up to her stout middle in water – and turned tail and walked with dignity – back to the kitchen. Nurse Matilda came to the edge of the pond and held out her hand, to help Cook ashore.

Cook was furious.

'Well! Just wait till Madam hears about *this*!' She stood, knee high in water, and you could see a week's notice written all over her face – in letters of mud. 'Let – me – tell – you, Nurse –' began Cook.

Nurse Matilda stood with her left hand held out; and with her right hand she raised her big black stick and gave a little thump. And almost before the thump had hit the ground, Cook's face had changed. 'Let me tell you, Nurse,' repeated Cook, taking the outstretched hand and hauling herself cheerfully up, 'that without those dear children, I don't know *where* I'd've been! Whatever come over me, I cannot imagine! Me toupee must have blown off – it often slips a bit: the Staff's quite used to it – and in running for it, I must have fell into the water. I'm not so nippy on me pins as I used to be,' admitted Cook, laughing good-naturedly. 'And those poor children must've all dived in and got theirselves wet, trying to help me out. Well, that *was* thoughtful of them! And I declare!' cried Cook, 'there's them good, kind dogs fetching me hair back to me!' Sure enough, Sugar had joined Spice and, having golloped up the sausages (little faces and all), they were now trotting quietly back, with Cook's hair carried delicately between them.

'So all's well that ends well,' said Nurse Matilda; and when the children had trooped into the house for hot baths and changes of clothes – closing every door carefully behind them, you can be quite certain – she went downstairs again and met Mrs Brown in the hall.

'Lesson Five,' said Nurse Matilda.

Chapter 7

HE children were very good all the next day, and even the Staff seemed softened by their experiences. Cook went to Mrs Brown and said that as Nurse thought the children should have a More Balanced Diet, however much she loved cooking roly-poly, and roast goose, with its thin, thin golden crackling, and swedes-in-butter (Speciality) and jellies and blancmanges – she would give it all up, and make boiled fish and rice-pudding so deliciously, that even they would like that just as much.

'I doubt if you – or even Nurse – will ever make them like greens,' said Mrs Brown.

'Well, perhaps not *greens*,' agreed Cook.

'I am sure they will just eat what they are given,' said Nurse Matilda, placidly; 'greens and all.'

And so they did. I can't say they liked the

greens, but all the rest was so nice that in the end they didn't mind a Balanced Diet a bit, and even began to be quite glad not to have to feel rather ill after every meal. And, of course, they were privately *very* glad about the jellies and blancmanges.

So the days went happily by and one day Nurse Matilda said, 'Well, children, it is my Day Off. Be very good and do exactly what you are told. And don't forget — *greens* for lunch!' and she put on her rusty black jacket and her rusty black bonnet with its trembles of jet, and took her big black stick, and stumped off down the drive.

So the children settled down to play, and after a while Mrs Brown came to the school-room and said, 'Children, where is Nurse Matilda?'

This is what the children were doing when Mrs Brown came to the schoolroom:

Helen had stirred mud into the mid-morning cocoa and they'd all taken huge big first gulps.

Nicolas had his hands drawn up into his sleeves and was prowling about being the Armless Wonder and frightening the Little Ones.

Lindy had redressed Little Justin with both legs in one trouser-leg and the poor boy was having to hop about like a robin.

Susannah had parachuted out of the window with an umbrella and landed in a manure heap : and now she was back again.

All the other children were being perfectly dreadful too.

Mrs Brown took one look at her dear children, armless, one-legged, choking up mud-and-cocoa and smelling of dung, and said, 'What a lovely time you seem to be having, darlings, but where is Nurse Matilda?'

So the children said, 'It's her day off. She's out.'

'Oh, dear,' said Mrs Brown. 'Well, darlings, your Great-Aunt Adelaide Stitch is coming to tea and she will wish to see you. So after lunch you must put on your best clothes.'

In the old days the children would have said to fat Nanny and the two starchy nurses and the governess – and even to their dear Mama, I'm afraid – 'Well, we jolly well won't.' But now they only grumbled and frowned and kicked the floor with the toes of their shoes (which is ruination to them) and growled out, 'Oh, *no*? *Need* we? We simply *hate* best clothes.'

'Poor darlings,' said Mrs Brown, 'but I'm afraid

you must. Aunt Adelaide Stitch is very rich and she's going to leave all her money to your papa and me, because she's so sorry for us, having such a lot of you. So it's only fair to be nice to her.' And she added, 'And don't kick the floor with the toes of your shoes, it's ruination to them,' and went away quite happy and confident in the good behaviour of her darling children.

The children had a splendid time after Mrs Brown had left them. They went down to the gate and lay in wait for the lad Podge, as he came out of school. You've heard of Podge before. Besides being the leader of the village gang, he was the only son of his mother and father, Mr and Mrs Green. Mr and Mrs Green kept the sweet shop in the village, so I suppose that's why Podge was so immensely fat. He was dreadfully greedy.

There were so many of the children, and Podge, being alone – he was always first out of school when the break-for-dinner bell rang – it was easy for them to capture him. They tied him up into a sort of bundle and hid him behind the hedge. By the time the other village children arrived, the Browns were all lolling about rubbing

their stomachs and crying out, 'Ow! Ow! Ow!'

'What's the matter?' said the village children, delighted to see the suffering Browns.

'We were warned never to eat Boy,' said the Browns, 'and now we have and the grown-ups were quite right: he's given us awful pains.'

'What Boy?' asked the village children.

'Podge Green,' said the Browns. 'We chose him because there was the most meat on him.' And they began to straighten up and lick their chops a bit and look rather significantly round at the other village children, as though singling out the next fattest.

The children took to their heels and ran, and soon Podge's father and mother came streaking down the street crying, 'What have you done with him? What have you done with our boy?'

'Gone!' said the children – which was quite true, because they had meanwhile released Podge, who had made off across the fields as fast as his stout legs would carry him. But they rubbed their stomachs in a meaningful sort of way and shook their heads mournfully as though they wished he *hadn't* gone – as though they wished they could have begun on him all over again, so delicious had he been.

'Gone?' cried Mr and Mrs Green, looking wildly about them.

'All gone,' said the children, regretfully.

'Or gog!' echoed the Baby, rubbing its tummy too.

'What – even that innocent child – ?' exclaimed Mr Green, staring in horror at the infant cannibal.

'It should still be on sieved vegetables,' cried Mrs Green, horrified too.

'And a little meat essence,' said Mr Green.

But the thought of meat essence and of their

poor boy boiled down to make it, was too much for the Podge parents. 'Help! Murder! Cannibalism!' they cried and, clutching at one another for support, they tottered off towards the police-station.

By the time Figgs, the village constable, had fully woken from his dinner-time nap (interrupted by the disturbing visit of Mr and Mrs Green), had run through his Police Manual for Instructions re Boy-eating in Rural Districts, and had buttoned up his uniform and found his helmet, Podge was back at his parents' home and was tucking into his middle-day dinner. (The meat, however, was pushed to one side of his plate.) Figgs saw the three of them as he passed on his way to the Browns', but he made no alteration in his purposeful progress. The boy Green had been reported Missing Believed Consumed by Cannibals; and Constable Figgs was going to investigate.

Hoppitt answered the door.

'I have come to Investigate,' said Constable Figgs.

'Investigate what?' said Hoppitt, smiling his superior, butler smile.

'Young Green,' said Figgs. 'Missing. Believed eaten.'

'Eaten?' cried Hoppitt, and his face quite lost its smile.

'Consumed on the premises, I understand,' said the constable, looking about him with interest.

'Follow me,' said Hoppitt, leading the way across the hall to the drawing-room. His mien was majestic still, but he was dreadfully pale. 'The C.I.D.,' he announced, flinging open the door and ushering the constable in; and he rushed off through the Baize Door to tell the rest of the Staff.

'Impossible!' cried Celeste. She said it in French, but it's the same word, anyhow.

'I wouldn't put it past them,' said Ellen, thinking it over.

'Had 'im for their dinner!' whispered Alice-and-Emily, aghast.

'After all them Balanced Meals!' said Cook.

Evangeline said nothing; but she glanced in the mirror at her own plump form and resolved to go on a diet from that moment on.

In the drawing-room, Constable Figgs had explained matters and Mr Brown had gone up to

the nursery to summon the children. ('But I'm sure,' said Mrs Brown, 'that they can't have done anything so naughty.') They filed in and stood in a ring on the drawing-room carpet.

'It 'as bin reported to me,' said Constable Figgs, looking down at them reproachfully, 'that you've ate up that young Green; had 'im for your dinner?'

'No, we haven't,' said the children. 'He was much too tough. Not Balanced enough, probably.' And they added, looking innocent, that they had only been doing exactly what they were told.

'What you were told?' cried Mrs Brown. 'Who ever told you to eat Podge Green?'

'Nurse Matilda,' said the children, respectfully.

'Gurk Magiggy,' said the Baby.

'Nurse Matilda! Told you to eat young Green –?' cried Constable Figgs.

'That's what she said,' said the children.

'Gack woggy keg,' said the Baby.

'But *what* did she say?' asked Constable Figgs and Mr and Mrs Brown, speaking all together.

'She said, "Green's for lunch",' said the children and the Baby, speaking all together too: only of course the Baby said, 'Geeng for gunk.'

'Green's for lunch!' said Constable Figgs: and he stood for a long time, quite still and quite silent, looking down at the toes of his big black boots. Then he took out his little black notebook and licked the lead of his big black pencil and wrote down: *Investigation into Outbreak of Cannibalism in Rural District*, and wrote after it in large black letters: CASE CLOSED; and closed the notebook too, and went away.

'There, you see!' said Mrs Brown, smiling happily at Mr Brown. 'I knew the children hadn't done anything so naughty.'

Chapter 8

ALL children have aunts and most children have at least one really fearsome aunt or even great-aunt. The Brown children had this truly fearsome great-aunt, Great-Aunt Adelaide Stitch.

Great-Aunt Adelaide Stitch was a terrible old person – very gaunt and tall, with an angry little eye like the eye of a rhinoceros. She had a nose a bit like a rhinoceros's too – like its horn, I mean, only of course it hooked downwards, not upwards like a horn. She knew the Catechism absolutely by heart, and she used to make the children stand in front of her – in their best clothes, of course – and recite it. Only, fortunately, there were so many of them that they never got beyond *What is your name?* because by the time they had got down to Arabella, Clarissa,

84

Sarah, Joanna, Timothy, Daniel, The Baby, the Tiny Baby, Sugar and Spice, she was worn out with the whole lot of them and didn't even go on to ask them *Who gave you your names?*

For some reason, Mr Brown was a little anxious about the afternoon ahead of them. 'I do hope the children will behave,' he said.

'Of course they will,' said Mrs Brown.

'What makes you think so?' said Mr Brown, rather gloomily for him. He was usually very cheerful, but he did sometimes worry in case Aunt Adelaide Stitch should go back on her promise to leave them all her money; because with such a lot of children, and so many people to look after them all, and such a big house to keep them all in, it did cost a dreadful lot. 'I wouldn't want the children to offend her,' he said, 'when – underneath – she's really so kind.'

'Oh, I'm sure they won't offend her,' said Mrs Brown.

'Well, what about last time?' said Mr Brown. 'When they tied ropes to her carriage, so when she started to drive away, graciously waving and bowing farewell to us, she found herself slowly going off backwards, across the lawn. And we had to pretend it was something wrong with the horses, and afterwards she spent hundreds of pounds sending them to the vet to be taught to go forwards again, and couldn't afford to give us any Christmas presents . . .' Which, he admitted, did serve the children right.

'They'll be good this time,' said Mrs Brown. 'Nurse Matilda has made them promise to do exactly as they're told.'

Up in the schoolroom, Ellen was having a difficult time while the children did exactly as they were told all through their lunch. When she said, 'Eat up your plates,' they all began taking great bites out of their plates, and when she said 'Pass the potatoes', they passed the potatoes but not the dish the potatoes were in; and when she said, 'Pass the butter-dish', they passed the dish but not the butter; and when she said (very thankful that the meal was at an end), 'Napkins folded, please!' – they all made a mad rush for the Tiniest Baby which was very happy to find itself suddenly waving its bare pink legs in the air . . . So she went away, rather desperate, only reminding them, 'Now, you are to put your best clothes on.'

'Who shall we *put* them on?' said Simon, when she had gone.

'Or *what* shall we put them on?' said Susie.

'Nobody's told us that,' said Christianna, thoughtfully. 'Ellen just said, "Put your best clothes on –" '

'I shall put mine on the hall table,' said Jaci. 'That'll be a nice welcome for Aunt Adelaide.'

'I shall put mine on the grand piano,' said Helen. 'Its round legs will look sweet in my frilly white drawers.'

'I shall put mine on Sugar,' said Caro, inspired.

'I kook gige og Pike,' said the Baby, before anybody else could.

'I shall put mine on Modestine,' said Susie. Modestine was their terribly grumpy donkey.

'I'll put mine on Aunt Pettitoes,' said Christianna. Aunt Pettitoes was, of course, the old mother sow.

'I'll put mine on Billy Goat,' said Simon.

'– On Nanny Goat,' said Francesca . . .

'We'll put ours on the hens,' said the Littlest Ones, happily. But it was Tora who won.

'I shall put mine on Evangeline,' she said.

'What a lot of noise the animals are making this

afternoon,' said Mr and Mrs Brown to one another as they awaited Aunt Adelaide's coming.

The vet had evidently been successful with Aunt Adelaide's horses, for they were pointing the right way and drew her carriage quite uneventfully up to the front door steps. She ascended with great grandeur, pausing only to bend over a perambulator which was standing in the sunshine outside the front door.

'Dear little mite! Thriving splendidly,' said Great-Aunt Adelaide, chucking the occupant of the perambulator under its rather beaky chin.

'Cluck, cluck, cluck!' said the occupant of the perambulator, from the depths of starched white embroidery. But after all, that is mostly what the occupants of perambulators do say. And Mr and Mrs Brown did not happen to glance in under the hood.

It was rather surprising to see a heap of white garments neatly folded on the hall table; and that each of the piano's well-turned legs seemed to be wearing a frill of starched white embroidery. But Aunt Adelaide's eyes were Not What they Used to Be – she was getting hard of hearing too – and she seemed to see nothing odd about it. Besides,

she was full of a new plan which she now
unfolded to Mr and Mrs Brown. She had been
thinking things over, she said, and had come to
the conclusion that Mr and Mrs Brown had too

many children – 'Oh, *no!*' cried Mrs Brown – and she had decided to take one of them, a nice, quiet, well–behaved gel (Aunt Adelaide always called girls 'gels') to live with her; so then they would have at least one less.

Poor Mrs Brown was appalled. Give up one of her dear, darling children to belong to Aunt Adelaide!

'But, Aunt –'

'No argument,' said Aunt Adelaide, raising a large, horny hand. 'I insist. Though no doubt you are overwhelmed by the benefits!' And she outlined the advantages the fortunate child would receive:

Her own suite of rooms, decorated in chocolate brown
A new wardrobe of clothing in colours that wouldn't show the dirt
A pug dog
A canary
A writing-desk
A work-box
And private tution in
   elocution,
   deportment,
   French,

German,
    Italian, and, above all, the pianoforte.

'Oh, but none of them could *bear* it!' sobbed Mrs Brown.

'What does she say?' demanded Aunt Adelaide, astounded.

'She says she couldn't bear it,' said Mr Brown, hastily. 'Parting with one of the children, she means.'

'Poof, nonsense!' said Aunt Adelaide. 'One out of so many? You'd never even miss her.'

'Aunt Adelaide you'd – you'd find that – well, that it wouldn't suit you.'

Aunt Adelaide's little rhinoceros eye began to grow red and angry.

'I may find that it doesn't suit me to leave you all my money when I die,' she said grimly. And she banged on the drawing-room carpet with her parasol – quite like Nurse Matilda, only in Aunt Adelaide's case nothing extra-ordinary happened.

'We shall now take a stroll about your grounds and observe your various daughters in, as it were, their natural habitat; and I shall choose one that appeals to me. I shall then take tea; China tea, if you please, and some thin brown bread and butter. By the time I am ready to leave, the chosen child will be waiting for me in my carriage, with a small bag packed with overnight wear. Otherwise,' said Aunt Adelaide, 'I shall be obliged to reconsider my Will.'

And she marched out with her little rhinoceros eye very beady and her large rhinoceros nose very set and determined; and down the front steps and into the garden. Mr and Mrs Brown followed her and simply didn't know what to do.

The children, meanwhile, had been struggling with the disposal of their best clothes. The hall table and the grand piano had been easy enough; but the pets and the farmyard animals were proving a little more difficult.

In those days, children's clothes were very stiff and starchy and frilly, and best clothes were usually white. The boys wore white sailor suits with round, white sailor caps and black silk scarves, and a whistle on a cord round their necks. The girls wore white embroidered dresses, very frilly, and several white petticoats underneath, very frilly too; and under the frilly white petticoats, frilly white drawers. And on top of the lot they wore frilly, round, white hats. I must say the poor things looked absolutely hideous.

And everything was starched: so starched that when it came back from the laundry the clothes were all stuck together and made a lovely sort of tearing-apart noise as you put your arm into a sleeve or your leg into a leg.

Sugar and Spice had put up with it fairly good-temperedly, and were now playing happily on the lawn. Mr and Mrs Brown saw them first and they held their breath. Aunt Adelaide peered across the grass at them, with her short-sighted eyes.

'A pretty pair,' she declared at last. 'But you have let them stay out in the sun too much. How dark their limbs appear, against their white clothes! And – can that be a piece of raw meat the little dears are playing with?'

Mr and Mrs Brown said in faltering accents that they didn't think it could be raw meat that the little dears were playing with – though in fact it was – and hurried Aunt Adelaide on. But their desperate glances said, behind her back, What on *earth* are the children up to now?

The children had got Aunt Pettitoes dressed at last, and though all her buttons wouldn't do up at

the back, she looked very well, standing with her two front feet on the wall of her sty, looking about her and grunting happily from beneath the rim of her floppy, round, white, embroidered hat.

But Nanny and Billy, the Goats, were being dreadfully difficult, as goats simply always are.

Billy had got Simon's trousers on all right, and the square, white sailor jacket, but Nanny, buttoned tightly into Francesca's dress, had immediately eaten his black silk scarf and then the cord of his whistle; and now by mistake she had swallowed the whistle as well and every time she breathed she went *Wheeeeeeeeee!*

And worst of all was Modestine. She really was a very grumpy donkey and cared for nothing but carrots; and certainly Susie's clothes were on the tight side for her, and the children had had to add some more clothes of the other children's – and Modestine was dreadfully uncomfortable.

The smaller children appeared to Aunt Adelaide, as she made her exploratory progress across the lawn, to be lolloping about in a very aimless fashion, tripping over their white dresses and chattering among themselves with a quite extraordinary mixture of hisses and clucks and bleats and grunts.

'You should bring in an elocution tutor at once,' she said to Mr and Mrs Brown. 'Their diction is disgraceful.' But anyway, they were all too small for her. 'Where are your older gels?' demanded Aunt Adelaide, beginning to grow a little suspicious that they were not going to be paraded for her to choose from. But, immediately, she caught sight of one of them, standing, quiet and well-behaved; just the sort of little girl she preferred. 'Let us go over and speak to her,' said Aunt Adelaide, waving with her parasol to where Aunt Pettitoes stood sunning herself, proud and pleased, in her white embroidered dress, with her little pink front-hooves propped up on the pigsty wall.

Oh *dear*!

Mr and Mrs Brown looked desperately at one another: there seemed to be no inspiration anywhere. And then – was that a glimpse of rusty black, motionless among the bushes at the edge of the shrubbery? – was that the faintest tinkle of jet, in a black bonnet? At any rate – inspiration came.

'Oh, I don't think she would suit you, Aunt Adelaide,' said Mr Brown, confidently.

'Why not?' asked Aunt Adelaide.

'She snores,' said Mr Brown, without a moment's pause.

'That will not signify. She will have her own suite of rooms. I shall not hear her at night.'

'But she snores all day too,' said Mrs Brown, just as inspired as Mr Brown; and certainly some very curious noises were coming from under the floppy white hat.

'Oh. Well, that's different,' said Aunt Adelaide, balked. She stopped in her tracks and stood looking about her: sniffing the air like a pointer scenting further prey. 'What is that curious whistling noise?'

The whistling noise was Nanny Goat, who now appeared galloping wildly round the corner from the stables, looking very odd indeed, it must be confessed, with her frilly hat caught up on one horn and her knickers coming down. And just when the Browns were praying that she would continue her mad career, she did just what goats always do – which is the thing you don't want them to do – and came to a sudden stop with all her four hooves bunched together, slap in front of Great-Aunt Adelaide; and stood there gazing up earnestly into her face. 'And which little gel are *you*?' said Aunt Adelaide, evidently rather taken by this flattering behaviour.

'Wheeeeeeeeeeeee!' went Nanny Goat.

'Severe asthma!' said Mr Brown, hurriedly. 'You wouldn't want –'

'I shall call in the Best Doctors,' said Aunt Adelaide. She gave Nanny a poke with her parasol. 'Stand up straight, dear, and answer properly when spoken to.'

In the ordinary way, Nanny Goat would, upon this, have taken to her heels and fled off across the grass; but of course she must do the wrong thing as usual, and to the horror of the Browns she got up on her hind legs, as ordered, and remained, as before, gazing earnestly into the old lady's face. The Browns stood paralysed, and prayed to hear once again that tiny, magic tinkle of jet.

Aunt Adelaide remained for one terrible moment gazing back at Nanny Goat. Then she gave her a second prod with the parasol and this time Nanny did take the hint.

'Poor child,' said Aunt Adelaide, watching her as she dashed off, tripping at every other step over the coming-down drawers. And she shuddered over the memory of it. 'Too sad, my dears! The little beard,' she said, shaking her head.

'Who is that Person?' asked Aunt Adelaide next, suddenly pointing with her parasol.

'What person?' asked Mr and Mrs Brown. They couldn't see anyone at all.

'An ill-favoured female, standing over there, in rusty black, with jet in her bonnet and a nose like two potatoes.'

'Whoever can it be?' said Mrs Brown. 'Has she got a Tooth?'

'Yes, a Tooth,' said Aunt Adelaide. 'And a large black stick.'

'Oh, it must be Nurse Matilda,' said Mrs Brown. 'How early she has come back from her day off!' But *she* couldn't see Nurse Matilda and neither could Mr Brown. 'Perhaps,' she said, 'she has gone round behind the stables.'

From behind the stables came a terrible 'Hee-haaaaaaaw! Hee-haaaaaaaaaaaaw! Hee-haaaaaaaaaaaaw!'

The children had got Modestine dressed at last, but they had to admit that she looked very odd. It had taken the best clothes of three of the girls to cover her, and even then her tail hung out at the back. Still, they had a floppy hat over each ear, and if only she'd kept her mouth shut, she'd have done very well. But she didn't. No longer able to kick out at them — for her legs were tightly buttoned into a petticoat apiece — she kept up her continuous, terrible braying; and now she had broken away from them and they knew that in half a minute she would be round the stables and out on the lawn in front of their advancing Mama and Papa and their Great-Aunt Adelaide; and though they didn't know about Aunt

Adelaide wanting one of them to take home with her, they did know about her leaving all her money to Papa and Mama when she died, and that she wouldn't if she was upset. And a chicken, two dachshunds, several geese, a pig and a goat, all dressed in starched white frillies, might so far have failed to upset Great-Aunt Adelaide; but they knew that Modestine and her dreadful hee-hawing was going too far. 'Oh, dear,' they said, 'if only Nurse Matilda were here!'

And suddenly – there she was! – black, trembly bonnet, nose, Tooth, stick and all.

'Why – what do you think *I* would do for you, you naughty children?' said Nurse Matilda; and she bit her lip and looked terribly stern.

'You might bang with your stick –?' suggested the children, hanging on to Modestine for dear life.

'That usually makes things worse,' said Nurse Matilda. 'Doesn't it?'

'Yes, it does,' said the children; and they looked unhappily at Nurse Matilda. And then they looked at her again. Was it possible – was it just possible that Nurse Matilda was biting her lip to keep herself from laughing?

'Well – we'll try,' said Nurse Matilda. And she

added, 'But not for your sakes, you naughty children! For your Papa's sake and Mama's.' And she banged with her big black stick on the stable floor.

But too late! At that moment Modestine broke away from their clutching hands and shot round the corner of the stable, floppy hats, starchy dresses, frilly petticoats and all — and, hee-hawing like a lunatic, dashed across the lawn, with all the children streaming after her, slap in front of Great-Aunt Adelaide. Great-Aunt Adelaide turned upon Mr and Mrs Brown with a face of outraged horror, her parasol raised in one gloved hand, the very figure of doom . . .

And in that second, Nurse Matilda's black stick once again came down on the stable floor; and Aunt Adelaide lowered her parasol, and to the amazement of Mr and Mrs Brown, there spread over her enraged features a smile which really was almost idiotic in its rapture.

'Why, what a merry game!' cried Aunt Adelaide, as Modestine swerved and went galloping across the grass, all the children in panic-chase behind her. 'What a charming-looking gel! See how prettily she sports with the

lads and lassies from the village – rough and ill-clad though they be! Hear her joyous laughter!' ('Hee-haw! Hee-haw!' went Modestine.) 'See! – now she dodges behind a bush! Now she has turned and pretends to run after *them* – how they all flee from her!' And she clasped her horny old hands in an ecstasy of delight, and turned upon Mr and Mrs Brown. 'This is the gel for me! I have not seen such spirit, such light-heartedness for many a long day. We can do with some of her gaiety at Stitch Hall.' And she clapped her hands and called out in silvery accents: 'Come here, dear! Come to me!'

'Hee-haw! Hee-haw!' went Modestine, galloping angrily after the children and nipping them sharply in the backs of their legs.

'She does not hear me. Come, dear!' called Aunt Adelaide, winningly. 'What is her name?' she said to Mrs Brown.

'Her – her name is Modestine,' said Mrs Brown.

'Come, Modestine!' called Aunt Adelaide.

'But I'm afraid she is really a – a donkey,' said Mr Brown.

'Nonsense,' said Aunt Adelaide, sharply. 'Just because the gel revels in a childish game, don't start calling her names . . .' But she was growing a little tired herself of the childish game. 'Bring her to me,' she said, imperiously. 'I have decided. This is the gel I shall choose!'

'But Aunt Adelaide –' began Mr Brown.

'But Aunt Adelaide –' cried Mrs Brown.

'No argument. If,' said Aunt Adelaide, 'Modestine is not in my carriage, bag packed and ready to depart, by the time I have had my cup of tea – not a penny piece of mine shall you ever see.' And she added: 'There is that Person again.'

And this time they did see her – Nurse Matilda, walking across the lawn towards them, still in her bonnet and rusty black jacket, as though she had only just that minute got back from her day off.

'Good evening, Madam,' she said, making a little bob in the direction of Aunt Adelaide; and to Mrs Brown she said: 'I am just this minute back from my day off. Is there anything I can do for you?'

'I am taking your Miss Modestine home with me,' said Aunt Adelaide, not letting Mrs Brown reply. 'I wish her to be ready, bag packed, and waiting in my carriage in a quarter of an hour from now.'

'Very well, Madam,' said Nurse Matilda; and she made a little bob again and went quietly away. Aunt Adelaide turned and hurried happily back to the front door.

A great quiet had fallen over house and garden. Dazed and apprehensive, not knowing what would happen, Mrs Brown poured out China tea for Great-Aunt Adelaide and pressed on her the brown bread and butter. Aunt Adelaide ate very little. She was far too excited and happy, reminding the bewildered Mr and Mrs Brown with her plans for dear Modestine's future:

A suite of rooms, my dears, decorated in chocolate brown

A whole new wardrobe of clothes in dark colours so

as not to show the dirt
A pug dog
A canary
A writing-desk
A work-box
And private tuition in
    elocution,
    deportment,
    French,
    German,
    Italian, and, above all, the pianoforte . . .

'And when she is of age,' concluded Aunt Adelaide, 'I shall single out a suitable young man for her to marry –' ('He will be an ass!' said Mr Brown under his breath, making a sort of awful joke of it, to try to cheer himself up.) '– I know the very young man, Adolphus Haversack, grandson of an old friend of mine. You need not fear for your legacy, my dears,' added Aunt Adelaide, seeing their anxious faces – which, however, were anxious for a very different reason: for how would they ever get Modestine into the carriage? 'She shall marry so well, that she'll need no money from me. It shall all come to you, for the happiness you have given me in allowing me

105

to take away this dear gel of yours.' And she looked out of the window and cried: 'Ah, there she is! Ready and waiting.'

And there she was – ready and waiting: sitting up in the carriage, not hee-hawing at all, simply sitting still, looking down modestly into her lap. Nurse Matilda stood respectfully by, with the little case of night-things all beautifully packed, in her hand.

Mr and Mrs Brown, standing wretchedly on the front steps as Great-Aunt Adelaide gaily mounted up into the carriage, looked distrustfully at Nurse Matilda. Could it be possible that this had been her way of helping? – that instead of urging Modestine into the carriage, she had sent off one of their own dear children? They tried to peer under the floppy white hat, but Modestine still hung her head – shedding a tear, perhaps, over the home she was leaving, for all the glories of the chocolate-coloured rooms and the lessons on the piano-forte? And – horror of horrors! – from the far-away stables came a sound that surely was 'Hee-haw! Hee-haw!' 'Aunt Adelaide –!' cried Mrs Brown, not able to bear the suspense one moment longer . . . But too late!

Clip, clop, clip, clop, went the horses' hooves: and the carriage had turned the corner of the drive and was out of sight.

'Nurse Matilda,' cried Mr and Mrs Brown, terrified, 'which of them –?'

From the stables came, 'Hee-haw; hee-haaaaaaaaaw . . .'

'Now then, Modestine,' Aunt Adelaide was saying, in the carriage. 'Look up and smile. I am sure you are going to be happy.'

'Oh, I'm sure I am,' said Modestine, looking up and smiling all over her face. 'Only –'

'Your own suite of rooms, Modestine; decorated throughout in chocolate brown . . .'

'Oh, thank you, how lovely!' said Modestine. 'Only –'

'A new wardrobe of dresses in dark colours so as not to show the dirt . . .'

'Oh, thank you,' said Modestine. 'Only –'

'And a pug dog –
And a canary –
And a writing-desk –
And a work-box –'

'How *lovely*,' said Modestine. 'Only –'

'– and private tuition in
elocution,
deportment,
French,
German,
Italian,
and,
above all,
the pianoforte . . .'

'Oh, thank you, Ma'am,' said Modestine, respectfully. 'Only –'

'You may call me Great-Aunt Adelaide,' said Great-Aunt Adelaide, graciously. And she added: 'Only – what?'

'Only you have my name a little wrong, Great-Aunt Adelaide. It's not *Modest*ine: it's *Evangel*ine.'

And so everyone was made happy. Great-Aunt Adelaide was happy because she had one of Mr and Mrs Brown's family (as she thought). And Evangeline was happy because she had the chocolate-coloured rooms and beautiful new dresses and the pug dog and the canary and the writing-desk and the work-box and all that private tuition. And Mrs Brown was happy because, although Aunt Adelaide had one of her children and was happy, she hadn't really got one of them, but she was still happy. And Mr Brown was very, very happy because he and his family would still have all Great-Aunt Adelaide's money when she died; which, however, he did most sincerely hope wouldn't be for many years to come, and, in fact, it wasn't – for Great-Aunt Adelaide lived to see Evangeline, beautiful and talented, united with that very Adolphus Haversack whom she had mentioned to Mr and Mrs Brown. And the Staff were happy for Evangeline's sake, who, however much put upon, had always been such a cheerful little lump; and they soon got another tweeny-maid and put upon her instead.

And night fell, and bedtime came: and Mrs Brown stood with Nurse Matilda at the nursery door.

'But why aren't the children asleep?' she said.

'Well, they are,' said Nurse Matilda.

'They're not in their beds?' said Mrs Brown.

'They're in the beds they have chosen,' said Nurse Matilda; and she smiled her own smile at Mrs Brown and said, softly: 'Lesson Six is almost over. Lesson Seven is about to begin.'

Chapter 9

WHERE Modestine – the real Modestine – slept that night, I don't know; though, no doubt, in her mysterious way, Nurse Matilda saw to it that she was comfortable – as comfortable as Aunt Pettitoes and Nanny Goat and Billy Goat and Sugar and Spice and the lambs and the geese and the hens. But where the children slept, I *can* tell you – for Susie slept in the stable, and Caro and the Baby slept curled up in the dog-basket, and Francesca and Simon slept in the goat pen, and some of the children slept among the geese, and some of them slept with the lambs, and the Littlest Ones nid-nodded on perches in the hen-house . . . Poor Christianna was the worst off – but, after all, nobody had *asked* her to change clothes with Aunt Pettitoes, had they?

And nobody had asked the other children to change with Modestine and the dogs and the goats and the geese and the hens.

But they had: and this was still Lesson Six.

I suppose it was because they were so uncomfortable that the children, that night, began to dream. At least it was a sort of dream. Afterwards they were never quite sure how much of it had been a dream and how much had been real. The dream was that at last – very, very early in the morning, almost before the sun was up – they all got up and went and met the others under the big beech tree on the lawn and said: 'This is too much. Let's run away.' And that suddenly, before they knew how it had happened, they *were* running away.

They couldn't stop it.

The house was very quiet. As they began to run, jogging across the lawn towards the drive and the big front gate, the windows seemed to frown down upon them, disapprovingly – those tall first-floor windows where, so long ago, they had mopped and mowed to frighten away the new nanny and nurses and the new governess, and the skinny little nursery-maid. They wished the house didn't seem so cross with them, standing there, frowning and silent, in the first faint light of the dawn, as though it were angry with them for wanting to leave it – for wanting to run away. But, in fact, they *didn't* want to run away. They'd run away often enough before, not caring two pins what the old house thought, never even considering that it might feel insulted and hurt, to be run away from; but this time it wasn't their fault – they didn't *want* to go.

And, what was more, they decided, suddenly, they weren't going to go, either – they were going to run back, they were going to run up the front steps and in at the front door and up to their own warm beds and never run away again . . .

They couldn't stop running, but they wheeled in their tracks and went back up the drive and up the front steps and pushed at the big front door.

It wouldn't open.

The door – their own, dear, old, welcoming, front door – it wouldn't open for them. And they couldn't stop – they had to keep on running. They ran down the steps again and down the drive; and as they ran, they thought: Perhaps the gate won't open either – and then we can't run away. We'll be safe. We'll just keep running round the garden till the grown-ups wake up and come down and stop us . . .

But, just as the front door wouldn't open – the gate wouldn't keep shut. As they approached it, it swung gently open, and – they couldn't help it, they couldn't stop – out they ran, and into the village street. And now they were really running away and there was nothing to be done about it but just to keep on.

They ran and they ran. The Big Ones ran first, the Littler Ones trailed after them, the Littlest Ones trailed after *them* – and last of all, the poor Baby, stumping along on its little bandy legs, as determined as ever not to be left behind. And all about them the village slept, the friendly doors of the little shops were shut, the closed eyes of the windows would not look at them as they passed. They came to the police-station and thought they saw the shadow of Constable Figgs on the blind (for we know that the Force Never Sleeps), and they called out, 'Constable Figgs, please come out and stop us!' but nothing happened and they called even louder, 'Come and stop us, arrest us, we've eaten up Podge Green!' If they were arrested, they thought, and thrown into prison, then they'd *have* to stop running; and soon their mother and father would come and bail them out.

But just as it seemed to them that the constable's shadow on the blind began to turn, as though he had heard and would do something about it, a window was slammed up and Podge

Green's fat, round face appeared and he cried out, 'No, they haven't eaten me! I wasn't a Balanced Meal!' and the window slammed down again, and the shadow on the blind didn't move any more; and the children ran on.

They ran on and on, and as they ran their feet went squildge, squildge, squildge in their boots: and they looked down, and all of a sudden it seemed to them in this strange half-dream that they had Wellington boots on – and the boots were full of treacle. So they tried to ease the boots off as they ran, but it was no use because

they had great big woolly grey socks on, too, and
the socks had been dipped in porridge and the
mixture of porridge and treacle was simply awful.
And they had their best clothes on, the boys in
white sailor suits and round sailor caps, and the
girls in their white embroidered dresses and frilly
round white hats. The starch scratched and
prickled as they ran, and the girls' hats fell down
over their eyes, and they couldn't see where they
were going. It didn't matter because they just had
to keep running, anyway.

And beneath the sailor caps and the round,

white hats, their poor faces were covered with large, round, painted spots; and they mopped and mowed as they ran. Sugar and Spice ran behind them, very gaily, dressed in brown Holland smocks and round, grey felt hats. The Baby, with its nappy coming down as usual, struggled along as best it could.

Out of the village, and into the country. The sun had not yet come up and it was grey and chilly in the flower-fresh, empty lanes. We shall run for ever, they thought. There'll be nobody here to stop us. But at that very minute they turned a corner and there, ahead of them, was – of all things! – a four-wheeler cab.

'Help, help!' cried the children. 'Stop us running! Stop us!'

'Yes, yes,' cried a voice from the cab, and a skinny little figure hopped out and came running towards them.

Help at last!

The skinny little figure ran towards them and they saw that it was a nursery-maid: you could tell she was a nursery-maid because she was so remarkably skinny. And if anyone would rescue them, *she* would. The skinny little nursery-maids were just as much put upon by the nannies and governesses and the starchy nurses as the tweeny-maids were by the Staff; but the children had always been friends with their nursery-maids.

'Oh, Sukey – Maria – Matilda – Mary-Ann,' cried the children, working backwards through all the long succession of nursery-maids. 'Oh, Maggie, Mary-Ann (again), Jemima, Jane – rescue us, save us, we want to stop running away . . . !' And they held out beseeching hands.

The skinny little nursery-maid stopped: stared: gave one startled squeak: and turned and ran back to the cab as fast as her skinny legs would carry her. Eight arms came out like an octopus and dragged her in.

'They're mad,' cried the skinny little nursery-maid. 'They're mopping and mowing! They're mad, and if they bite us we'll go mad too!'

Five alarmed faces gazed out of the back window as the cab galloped wildly away. Sighing sadly, the children ran on; and mopped and mowed as they ran.

The dawn came and still they were running. Justin had both feet in one trouser leg, poor boy, and was hopping along like a robin, Tora had sold all her legs and arms and the Baby was staggering about among the children as they loped along, holding out the little nursery potty and calling, 'Alms for ge luvvy Aggy!' – trying to collect enough to buy them back for her. And every child had a stitch by now, and cried out as it ran, 'Ow my *stitch*!'

'Stitch?' cried a great voice, high and hooting, booming back. 'Who calls for Adelaide Stitch?'

'Aunt Adelaide,' cried the children. 'Save us! Save us!'

Great-Aunt Adelaide Stitch appeared round a corner. She had Evangeline on one side of her, dressed up very finely in dark clothes, not to show the dirt; and on the other a tall young man with large brown eyes, wearing a tight checked suit and curly bowler of the utmost expensiveness.

'This is Adolphus Haversack,' said Aunt Adelaide. 'Dear Evangeline's intended.'

'Oh, Adolphus Haversack,' cried the children, checking their headlong rush, but still having to jog up and down, running on the spot, 'please save us!'

'If anyone can do so,' said Aunt Adelaide, 'it will be Adolphus. He is Exceedingly Rich.'

Adolphus Haversack took off his curly bowler and bowed deeply. 'Anything Miss Evangeline commands,' he said in a voice of silver – everything about Adolphus Haversack was expensive, even his voice – 'anything Miss Evangeline commands, I will do.'

'Evangeline,' cried Great-Aunt Adelaide Stitch, imperiously. 'Command him!'

'Hee-haw,' said Evangeline.

'Hee-haw?' said Adolphus Haversack, startled and suprised.

'Hee-haw,' said Evangeline.

'Come, Evangeline,' said Aunt Adelaide. 'Don't be a little donkey, dear. Talk horse sense.'

'Hee-haw,' said Evangeline.

The children, marking time, jerked up and down and gazed imploringly at Evangeline. Poor Justin was still hopping. Tora had bought back one leg and both of her arms, thanks to the efforts of the Baby, and though somewhat lop-sided, was managing better.

'Evangeline,' they begged. 'Do please command him!'

Evangeline shook her head and her ears rattled. 'Evangeline,' insisted the children, 'if you'll only ask him –'

'– they will give you –' said Aunt Adelaide.

'– a pug dog,' cried the children, jogging up and down anxiously.

'And a canary,' said Aunt Adelaide.

'Yes, and a writing-desk –'

'– and a work-box.'

'Oh, yes and a work-box. And private tuition in –'

'– elocution –' said Aunt Adelaide.

'– and deportment –'

'– and French, German and Italian –'

'– and, above all,' promised the children –

'– lessons in the pianoforte,' finished Aunt Adelaide triumphantly. 'There, Evangeline – what do you think of that?'

'Hee-haaaaaaaaaw,' said Evangeline; and she kicked up her heels and bolted. Aunt Adelaide Stitch picked up her long skirts and bolted after

her. Adolphus Haversack twirled his stick and followed them languidly. The children's feet stopped marking time and started to run again.

On and on and on.

The sun came up and dried the sparkly dew on the hedgerows, and breakfast time came and went, and they were hungry and thirsty, but there was nothing to eat or drink, and no time to stop, if there had been, to eat and drink it. At mid-morning, they thought they smelt lovely, steaming cocoa; but it was only a little stream running under a bridge, and the cocoa was made with mud. And when dinner-time came, they caught a whiff of steak-and-kidney pudding and, sure enough, there it was, great platefuls of it spread out on a table by the wayside, with a great dish of golden roly-poly beside it. But as, streaming by, they reached out their hungry hands to grab some, a huge cardboard notice came down like a guillotine between the plates and their hands, saying GOING TO WASTE ON ACCOUNT OF MEASLES. From behind the bushes, as they ran, came a chorus of throaty giggling, and out between the roots of the hedgerows poked little, jeering, sausage faces, and they saw, now, that the flowers in the hedgerows weren't flowers at all, really, but dabs and blobs of white blancmange and pink jelly. They'd have welcomed even jelly and blancmange by now, but they couldn't stop to pick any – they had to keep on running.

The long day passed – the long, long, weary day. At tea-time, they thought they saw a gleam of silver up on the hillside, where a tiny river started off on its life's journey; but it was tea, really, pouring down the hillside from a huge brown nursery teapot, and just as they came up to it, gasping, there was another huge brown teapot by the roadside, and the tea all flowed back into it and disappeared, and the lid went on with a *clop*! and they couldn't stop to get it off. 'We can't run any more,' said the poor children, desperately. 'We can't!' But they had to. They just couldn't not run.

Evening came. They breasted the top of a hill and saw Aunt Pettitoes sunning herself there in the dying light, her front hooves elegantly crossed as she leaned on a low wall.

'Look, dears,' said Aunt Pettitoes to her piglets as the children trailed past her, 'there are the children, running away!'

'Aunt Pettitoes, stop us, save us,' cried the children. 'We don't *want* to be running away.'

'Pooh, nonsense,' said Aunt Pettitoes. 'I know you children – you're always running away.'

'You're unkind and horrid and your babies look like vegetable marrows,' cried the children, resentfully, 'and you look jolly silly yourself, in that frilly round hat.'

But they still had to keep on running. They passed Billy and Nanny, and a gaggle of geese, and their friends the speckled hens: but the goats and the geese and the hens were all busy trying on sailor suits and frilly dresses and took no notice of a long file of children wearily jog-trotting by.

And then, suddenly – hope again! They seemed to have run all day between nothing but deserted country lanes. But now there was a village in sight.

Weary, failing, hungry and thirsty, on tottering legs the children streeled into the village, strung out in a straggling line – the Big Ones leading, plodding doggedly on, the Middlings trailing behind them, the Little Ones stumbling after *them*, dragging the Littlest ones by small, hot, unwilling hands: the Baby still gamely staggering along at the very end, with its nappy round its fat, bent knees. Sugar and Spice still frisked at their heels, wearing the Holland smocks and the round grey hats. (*They* weren't being taught any lesson, they were only little dogs: someone – Someone – was seeing to it that Sugar and Spice didn't feel or suffer as the naughty children must.)

The curtains were drawn in the little village street, the lamps were beginning to be lit. For dusk had fallen. The children had been running the whole day long.

Wearily, wearily they jog-trotted into the lamp-lit street.

'Save us!' they cried to the curtained windows, where the warm lights glowed.

'Of course!' cried a hundred voices from within. 'Of course we will!'

Squeaky voices, growly voices, ol'-man-river voices: short, sharp, barking-out-orders voices . . . Dolls' voices, teddy bears' voices, golliwogs' voices, the voices of tin soldiers . . . The voices of the children's toys!

'We're safe at last, cried the children. 'The toys will rescue us.'

And the curtains parted and windows slammed up and the toys poked out their heads . . .

And chop, chop, chop! – a scatter of wax, of sawdust, of cotton-wool stuffing, of broken lead – and the heads fell plop, plop, plop! into the village street.

The toys would have rescued the children; but long ago Nicolas had executed them all.

And so, despair in their hearts, the children ran on.

But now . . . It was a very strange village. For now the main street ended suddenly – in a huge, big, green Baize Door.

They needn't go any farther. They just couldn't. They wouldn't be *able* to run any more. The Baize Door barred their way.

And here were Hoppitt and Cook and Celeste and Alice-and-Emily standing before the Baize Door; and crying out with one voice, 'Lawks a mussy! – who's this?'

'Oh, Hoppitt! Oh, Cook!' cried the children, faint with thankfulness. 'It's the children. It's *us*!'

At least, that's what they meant to say. But what do you think came out? 'Oh, Humps-mumps! Oh, Cumps! Dumps the Chumps-mumps! Dumps *umps*!'

'Foreigners!' cried Hoppitt, and flung wide the door and stood aside: and slowly, wearily, but inexorably, the children's legs began to carry them through and out on the road again. 'Stop us! Stop us!' cried the children, desperately, clutching at the last straw. But it came out as 'Stumps umps!' and Hoppitt only added, 'Foreign cricketers at that; we don't want the likes of them here,' and flattened himself against the open Baize Door to let them pass.

'They look tired, poor things,' said kind Alice-and-Emily, and bent to peer into their faces. 'And all them spots!' they added, pitifully.

'Spots?' shrieked Celeste.

'Fetch the medicine,' cried Cook.

'Fetch the brooms, you mean,' screamed Celeste. 'Fetch the mops, fetch my curling tongs. It's the Measles. We don't want the Measles here!'

And nip, nip, nip went the curling tongs, and swish went the brooms and bang went the mops; and the children were through the door and out on the long, chill, darkling road again; and the stars came out and it was night. And they ran and they ran . . .

And suddenly – the Baby fell down. It tripped over its nappy at last, and stumbled and fell; and it sat in a round, mournful bundle in the middle of the road and just couldn't get up. And at last put its fat round fists in its eyes and sobbed out: 'Nurk Magiggy. Wonk Nurk Magiggy! Wairg my Nurk Magiggy?'

And a voice said out of the darkness, and as

velvet as the darkness, 'Darling Baby: I am here.' And out of the darkness came two arms and caught up the Baby against a loving shoulder and held it close.

And all the children stopped running at that moment and cried out, 'Oh, why didn't we think of it before? Nurse Matilda – come to us!'

And the voice said: 'Yes, children. Yes, darlings. I am here.'

And in that one moment – how could it have happened that to each child it seemed as if those loving arms came around him and he was lifted up gently and his weary head cradled against a kind shoulder? And he was carried softly and silently through the night and slipped into his own warm, cosy bed at home: washed and brushed and changed into pyjamas, teeth cleaned, prayers said and peacefully dreaming . . .

Dreaming that he was running away: but would wake up in his bed in the morning, all safe and sound – only quite, quite certain never to run away again.

For that had been Lesson Seven.

Chapter 10

THAT afternoon Mrs Brown said to Nurse Matilda, 'It is too dreadful, but a friend of mine called Mrs Black is coming this afternoon, and she will want to see the children.'

So Nurse Matilda said to the children, 'A friend of your Mama's, called Mrs Black, is coming this afternoon and will wish to see you. Wash your hands and faces and put on your best clothes and go down to the drawing-room.' And she lifted her big black stick as though she were about to give one thump on the floor with it; and changed her mind and just added calmly, 'Please, children.'

So the children went upstairs and washed their hands and faces and put on their best clothes and went down to the drawing-room and sat down quietly in a ring all round their Mama and Mrs

Black. And Mrs Black said, 'I never *saw* such well-behaved children.'

'Aren't they?' said Mrs Brown, beaming. She had never for one moment really thought her children were naughty.

'When I left home,' said Mrs Black, 'this is what *my* children were doing:

Emma had put a piglet in the baby's cot and sent for the doctor.

Lucy'd filled the loo with sticks and coal and lit a fire in it.

Thomas had tied the twins' plaits together behind their heads, and they couldn't get apart.

Victoria had covered little William with squished-up tomatoes to be a Red Indian, and put on his clothes on top of it.

And all my other children were doing simply dreadful things too.'

And Mrs Brown and all the children said with one voice, 'The person *you* need is Nurse Matilda.'

And then the children added, very quickly: 'Only you can't have her. She's ours.'

Nurse Matilda stood in the doorway and she smiled. She smiled and she smiled – but yet, at the same time, two big tears gathered in her eyes and rolled down her cheeks. And as they rolled – they seemed to roll away the very last of Nurse Matilda's wrinkles. And her face wasn't round and brown any more, and her nose, like two potatoes, was changing its shape altogether: and even her rusty black clothes seemed to be getting all goldeny. And when Mrs Black whispered to Mrs Brown, 'But she's so *ugly*!' Mrs Brown whispered back in astonishment, 'How can you say so? She's perfectly lovely!'

But Nurse Matilda's two tears rolled on down her face; and she said to Mrs Brown, 'I told you.'

'Told me what?' said Mrs Brown; and all the children cried out, 'Told her what?' and then corrected themselves and asked politely, 'Please tell us what it was you told Mama.'

And Nurse Matilda said, 'I told her that when you didn't need me – but you did want me: then I must leave you.' And all the children burst out crying and said, 'Oh, no, don't leave us – don't leave us . . .!'

And Nurse Matilda smiled through her tears and said, 'I don't want to – I've loved you all so much, you really have been far, far the naughtiest

of *all* my children . . .' And her smile was so lovely
that she would have looked like the loveliest
person in all the world if only – well, even the
children and Mrs Brown had to admit it – if only
it hadn't been for that terrible Tooth! And at that
moment, just as they were thinking it – couldn't
help thinking it – she gave one last thump with
her stick on the ground and – what do you think
happened? That Tooth of hers flew out, and
landed on the floor at the children's feet.

And it began to grow.

It grew and it grew. It grew until it was the size
of a match-box. It grew until it was the size of a
snuff-box. It grew until it was the size of a shoe-
box – of a tuck-box – of a suit-case – of a

packing-case – of a trunk: of a big trunk, a huge trunk, a simply enormous trunk. . . . And suddenly the trunk flew open and, inside, it was crammed to the top, full up, bursting, bulging out at the seams with toys – the most marvellous toys you ever saw. And the more toys they took out of it, the more toys seemed to remain to be taken out: not one toy for each child, not two toys for each child, but dozens and dozens of wonderful toys for every single child in the whole Brown family . . .

When they all had their toys and at last the trunk was empty and they looked up again – Nurse Matilda was gone.

NURSE MATILDA
GOES TO TOWN

To Simon Taylor
my godson

NCE upon a time there were a mother and father called Mr and Mrs Brown and they had a huge family of children; and all the children were terribly, terribly naughty.

One day Mrs Brown went up to the schoolroom to speak to her children and this is what they were doing:

Tora had put glue in the sandwiches.

Emma had made a large chocolate cake out of mud.

David had put a toad in the milk-jug – and Tim was under the table tying Nanny's feet to the legs of her chair with her shoe-laces. All the other children were doing simply dreadful things too.

Mrs Brown was very sweet, but she really was rather foolish about her darling children and never believed that they could possibly be naughty. So she said, 'Good afternoon, Nanny. I hope you are all enjoying your tea?'

Nanny was having a terrible time with her false teeth because of the glue in the sandwiches. She tried to say, 'Stand up, children, and say good afternoon to your dear Mama,' but it came out, 'Mmph, mmph, mmph . . .' She stood up, herself, to give a good example and fell flat down on the table because of her tied-up legs, with her face in the mud cake. At that moment the toad got tired of the milk-jug and took one huge leap out of it and landed on top of her head. Wearing him like a little mottled hat, she raised her poor, mud-clotted face to Mrs Brown, gave her one long, baleful look and, with the chair still tied to her, hopped and hobbled out of the room. Mrs Brown knew that look very well. It meant that she was going to have to go to the Agency and get another new Nanny for her darling children.

Some of *you* darling children will have read about how Nurse Matilda once came to the Brown family and made them all good and well-behaved. She was terribly ugly when she arrived, but as they got gooder and gooder, so she had become prettier and prettier, until she ended up quite lovely and all surrounded in a sort of golden glow. I'm afraid the children had slipped back very badly since then; and as if she hadn't got enough, Mrs Brown had gone out and adopted several more and they were just as naughty as their new brothers and sisters. Even she began to think that it would be a good idea if Nurse Matilda could come back and begin all over again.

Especially as . . .

Especially as the children were all going to stay with their Great-Aunt Adelaide, in town.

Most children have at least one fearsome aunt or even great-aunt. The Brown children had this truly fearsome great-aunt, Great-Aunt Adelaide Stitch.

'Now, children,' said Mrs Brown, 'I have some news for you. Your papa and I are going abroad for a holiday and you are all going to stay with Aunt Adelaide Stitch.'

The children would all have burst into most terrible exclamations of horror, but they couldn't because of the glue in the sandwiches; and Mrs Brown beamed round upon them and went happily back to the drawing-room. 'The children

are speechless with pleasure,' she said to Mr Brown. 'Oh, dear,' groaned Mr Brown, glumly. He had less faith than Mrs Brown and he thought that the children had probably already got plans for being naughty at Great-Aunt Adelaide's. Great-Aunt Adelaide was very rich and she was going to leave him all her money when she died. He didn't want her to die a bit, but when she did the money would come in very handy. He really did have so many children.

The children were by no means speechless when at last they got free of the glue. 'It's too *horr*ible!' they said. 'It'll be *aw*ful! And she lives in

*Lon*don!' 'Ick *hog*gigig,' echoed the Baby. 'Ickle-ge *ork*ig! Anke livinging *Gung*-king!' It was a splendid baby and talked a language all of its own.

Great-Aunt Adelaide Stitch was a terrible old person – very gaunt and tall, with an angry little eye like the eye of a rhinoceros and a nose like the horn of a rhinoceros, turned upside-down. She lived in a big house, as tall and gaunt-looking as herself, with a neat London garden round it with green cardboard lawns and all the flowers marshalled in their beds like soldiers on parade. With her, nowadays, lived Evangeline. Evangeline had once been the poor little tweeny-maid in the Browns' home in the country. Great-Aunt Adelaide Stitch had tried to adopt one of the Brown children and somehow had managed to get Evangeline instead. Fortunately Evangeline enjoyed living with her very much, because at least it was better than being a put-upon tweeny-maid; and she now had, as promised by Aunt Adelaide at the time of her adoption:

Her own suite of rooms decorated in chocolate brown, a huge wardrobe of absolutely hideous clothes which, however, they both thought most beautiful, and –

A pug dog

Aunt Adelaide

Evangeline

A canary
A writing-desk
A work-box
And private tuition in
elocution
deportment
French
German
Italian, and, above all, the pianoforte.

She had profited greatly from all these benefits and by now, I'm afraid, instead of being a cheerful little lump, she had become a stout little, horrid little prig. But she was just exactly what Great-Aunt Adelaide liked.

Evangeline was standing at the front door when the children arrived in a fleet of four-wheeler cabs; her pug was beside her and they were both looking forward eagerly to welcoming their guests. (The pug had a most original name: it was Pug – that was the kind of girl Evangeline was; her canary was called Canary. But still she had the example of Great-Aunt Adelaide before her. Great-Aunt Adelaide had a parrot and its name was Parrot.)

The children had brought their two

dachshunds, Sugar and Spice, and the looks on their faces when they set their bright, twinkly eyes upon Pug, made Pug's welcome a lot less eager.

There were so many children in Mr and Mrs Brown's family that we never have got round to writing down all their names; especially now, with the extra adopted ones. Even their own mother and father had to divide them into the Big Ones and the Middling Ones and the Little Ones and the Tinies. There was also the Baby and the Littlest Baby and now there was a Littler Baby Still, but the last two babies couldn't walk or talk, so they really were rather dull. The oldest baby talked a language all of its own, as we have seen. It wore a rather bundly collection of nappies which always seemed just about to fall down, but never quite did.

They all climbed out of the cabs as Evangeline stumped down the front door steps to greet them, with Pug on one side of her and Miss Prawn on the other. Miss Prawn was her governess. Summer and winter she suffered dreadfully from chilblains on her poor, thin hands.

'Oh, the pretty dears! How charming!' cried

Miss Prawn, clasping the chilblains as the children closed the doors of the cabs, gave the horses a pat to say thank you, and marched in a grumpy crocodile up to the front door. In fact they looked anything but charming, being dressed in their hideous second-best clothes for travelling. Many of them carried closed matchboxes in their hands.

At home in the country, the Brown family had lots of outdoor animals and most of the animals had fleas, especially the goats. The children had brought with them several fleas, willingly surrendered by the goats, and housed carefully in the matchboxes, lined with animal hair so that they should not feel the journey too badly. They had had an idea that something of the sort might come in useful, at Aunt Adelaide's house: and the moment they set eyes on Pug, they knew they had been right.

Pug and Evangeline led them into the hall, which was very tall and bleak, and they stood round in a resentful circle, longing only to jump back into the four-wheeler cabs, and go home. But Simon gave them a wink and bent down and patted Pug. 'What a dear little dog!' he said. 'Only,' he added, opening his matchbox and giving the contents a shake all over Pug, 'he has fleas.'

The children set up a terrible hullabaloo. 'Ow, ow!' they cried. 'Fleas! Don't let him come near *us*!'

Miss Prawn was overcome with horror and disgust. 'Nonsense! What indelicacy! Dear Pug has no such thing!'

'But look!' said Charlotte, secretly opening *her*

matchbox and pointing to a large flea which had hopped out on to Pug's broad back, and was looking about itself joyfully, hoping Pug would turn out to be a goat.

'Ow, ow!' screamed the children. 'It's another flea!' And they all started scratching like mad and picked up Sugar and Spice and held them out of harm's way. 'Don't let him give fleas to our lovely clean dogs!'

'Pug is perfectly clean,' protested Miss Prawn, scandalized.

'He isn't, he's covered in fleas and now we're covered in fleas too,' cried the children, hopping up and down, scratching themselves. 'And so are you, Miss Prawn — you've got one on your arm.'

And sure enough, a third flea was stretching its hind legs on the fuzzy brown serge of Miss Prawn's sleeve, and this one was quite sure that it was back on a goat. 'Ow, ow, ow!' cried Miss Prawn, and started hopping and scratching too. 'Ow, ow, OW!' cried Evangeline, not even waiting to be flea-ridden before setting up a hullabaloo; and suddenly squealed out: 'Oh, Aunt Adelaide — what do you think? Pug's got fleas!'

For Great-Aunt Adelaide Stitch, ear trumpet and all, had appeared at the turn of the stairs. 'Fleas?' she said, in her high, hooting voice. '*Fleas?*'

'Yes, fleas,' cried the children. 'He's covered in fleas, we're all covered in his fleas, we shall have to go home.' And they started scratching and hopping and wriggling again. Miss Prawn was dancing frantically, holding her arm out stiffly before her, Evangeline wobbling like a jelly with imaginary itching, Sugar and Spice shrilly barking, the wretched Pug lugubriously howling. 'Miss PRAWN!' shrieked Great-Aunt Adelaide into all this tumult. 'What is happening? What's the meaning of this?'

'Pug's got fleas,' yelled the children. They set up a sort of chanting. 'Pug's – got – *fleas*. We'll – all – have to go – *home*. Pug's – got – *fleas*. We'll – all – have to go – *home* . . .' 'It's fleas,' faltered Miss Prawn. 'On Pug.'

'Fleas?' screeched Aunt Adelaide, over the din. 'I don't believe a word of it. How can he have fleas?'

'It's no fault of mine. He has his weekly bath,' said poor Miss Prawn. She held out a trembling brown serge arm. 'I have one too.'

Aunt Adelaide's eyes nearly popped out of her head. 'I am not interested in your personal habits, Miss Prawn.'

'I didn't mean *I* have a weekly bath,' said Miss Prawn, still holding out her arm.

'Then you ought to. Most insanitary! This is doubtless where all the trouble has arisen. Blaming a poor, innocent little dog, when all the time . . . SILENCE!' yelled Great-Aunt Adelaide suddenly over the hopping and chanting of the children. She descended the stairs, hitting out wildly at the bobbing heads with her ear trumpet. 'Be quiet, all of you! Stop hopping! Nothing serious has happened. No one is going home.' She added in a voice of doom: 'Except Miss Prawn. Prawn, you may depart. You are dismissed.'

Miss Prawn dropped her brown serge arm to her side, flea and all, and stood staring up at Great-Aunt Adelaide, with her face turned as pale as ashes. 'Dismissed? But I can't . . . You can't . . . My poor old mother,' whimpered Miss Prawn, 'she needs the money I give her. And I, myself — where could I go?'

'Wherever you go,' said Aunt Adelaide, 'it will be without a reference.' She gestured majestically up the stairs with her ear trumpet. 'Up to your room and pack your bags! Be gone!'

Absolutely silent, absolutely still, the children watched the meagre figure in its dull brown serge creep up the stairs. But they knew that it couldn't be allowed: they knew that they must confess. What would happen to them when they did, they could not imagine — sent back home in disgrace, poor Mama and Papa recalled from their holiday, Great-Aunt Adelaide ordering out her carriage and galloping round to the lawyer's to alter her will . . . But still, they couldn't let Miss Prawn be sent away. Standing there in their suddenly silent ring, with Evangeline and Pug huddled, scared and miserable, in the middle, the Big Ones exchanged glances: passed the word on silently to the Middling Ones: nodded to the Littlies. Their hearts felt faint and fluttering, but it had to be said. 'Aunt Adelaide —' they began . . .

'Arnk Aggigaige —' said the Baby.

'It isn't Miss Prawn's fault,' said the children. 'You see —'

And there came a knocking at the big front door. And all of a sudden it seemed to open all by itself and someone stood there before it, as it quietly closed. And a voice said: 'The Agency has sent me, Madam. I am Nurse Matilda.'

The Agency has sent me, Madam.

Chapter 2

AND there she was – Nurse Matilda! – with her bun of hair sticking out at the back of her head like a teapot handle, and her wrinkly round face and two little, black, boot-button eyes. And her nose! – her nose was like two potatoes! She wore a rusty black dress right up to her neck and down to her black button-boots; and a rusty black jacket and a rusty black bonnet all trimmed with trembly black jet. And she carried a very big black stick. What Nurse Matilda could do with that big black stick!

But what you noticed most of all about Nurse Matilda was her Tooth – one huge front Tooth, sticking right out like a tombstone over her lower lip . . .

The children all swung round towards the door and stood there, rooted to the spot, staring. Only the Baby stumbled forward on its fat, bent legs with its nappies falling down, and cried out: 'Nurk Magiggy! Ick my Nurk Magiggy!' The children started to say: 'Yes, it is; it's Nurse Matilda . . .' But somehow the words got stuck in their throats and they found themselves saying to each other instead: '*Who* is it? What is the Baby trying to say?'

All their memories of Nurse Matilda had gone right out of their heads.

But the Baby – the Baby still toddled on; and Nurse Matilda put out a brown, speckled hand and took the Baby's own confiding fat little hand and stood there, holding it. She said to Aunt Adelaide: 'The Agency, Madam, suggested that you might be needing me.' And she looked up at the trembling, brown-clad figure on the stairs. 'To assist Miss Prawn.'

Great-Aunt Adelaide pushed her way through the throng of puzzled children. 'Quite correct. I do indeed need someone. Miss Prawn, however, is leaving.'

Nurse Matilda stood with the Baby's rose-leaf hand in hers. 'I am sorry, Madam. The Agency positively stated that I should assist Miss Prawn.'

She released the Baby's hand and turned to go. 'I am sorry to have troubled you needlessly.'

'Nonsense!' said Aunt Adelaide. 'You will remain here.'

'Certainly, Madam – to assist Miss Prawn.'

'Very well, very well,' said Aunt Adelaide, ungraciously. 'You had better both stay. But I warn you,' she added, 'Miss Prawn is infested. She has fleas. She will have to be Dealt With.'

'I shall deal with *every*body, Madam,' said Nurse Matilda; and some sort of shadowy memory seemed to suggest to the children that she probably meant it.

Upstairs, the fleas took one look at the large, chilly rooms set apart for the children, and apparently took a dislike to them; for they hopped back all by themselves into one of the matchboxes and settled down into a little refugee community, grieving for home – which in their case was a large brown goat. The children didn't very much like the rooms either, and they, also, longed for home. Only Miss Prawn seemed blissfully happy to be able to remain with her dear pupil Evangeline, and give Pug his weekly bath.

Nurse Matilda, however, stood no nonsense and soon all the clothes were unpacked and put away in two long dormitories arranged for the boys and the girls; and they collected in Evangeline's schoolroom for tea – which was absolutely horrible, bread and butter and a very solid dark red plum jam, and some extremely dull currant buns. 'After tea,' they said, 'we'll go out into the garden and play some games.'

'After tea,' said Miss Prawn, 'I had thought of a little concert. Evangeline will play her piece —'

'And you will give us one of your songs, Miss Prawn?' cried Evangeline. 'How lovely!'

How ghastly! thought the children; it was gloriously sunny outside.

But Evangeline dashed to the piano and Miss Prawn stepped forward and announced in romantic accents a song called *Prince of My Dreams* and, flinging out her hands towards the children as though inviting them to have a closer look at the

chilblains, opened her mouth. Out of it came a long, high wail like a dog in deep distress.

Miss Prawn, looking somewhat distressed herself, shut her mouth hurriedly; waited a second, opened it again and tried once more. Out came another howl, even higher and longer than the first. Evangeline, banging away at the piano, looked round and nodded encouragement. She evidently thought it all most beautiful.

Sitting cross-legged all round the room, the children stuffed their fists into their mouths to stifle their giggles. For the fact was that Roger had Pug by the tail and was teasing him with a bit of left-over bun.

Pug was a greedy dog and every time the bun disappeared, he howled – and every time it disappeared happened – most strangely – to be

every time Miss Prawn opened her mouth to sing. The poor thing had really got going at last, but she did seem astonished at the sounds that appeared to be coming out of her. 'Pri-hince of my dreeeeeeeams,' she warbled, holding out the chilblains again, and 'Ow-wow-wooooooooow,' wailed Pug. Tears of happiness rolled down Evangeline's cheeks, it was all so beautiful; tears of laughter rolled down the children's, with the effort not to laugh out loud. Sugar and Spice, who couldn't bear music anyhow, opened their mouths and joined in; and Miss Prawn, more and more astounded at the sounds she was making, was evidently beginning to wonder whether she shouldn't have gone in for being an opera singer, after all. Nurse Matilda's beady black eyes looked round upon her charges.

By the end of the song they were beginning to get a little weary of it; the noise really was frightful and it was so nice and sunny out of doors. 'Last chorus!' cried Evangeline, over her shoulder to Miss Prawn, and, 'Thank you, Miss Prawn,' began the children, scrambling to their feet all ready to dash out into the garden the moment it was over.

But it wasn't over. For Nurse Matilda banged just once on the schoolroom floor with her big black stick; and Jennifer found herself, to her own horror, begging: 'Do please sing it again!'

This time Sugar and Spice and Pug needed no urging. They sat in a ring round Miss Prawn and lifted up their heads and howled; and Miss Prawn lifted up *her* head and howled, and Evangeline pounded away at the piano like a mad thing, crimson with happiness at finding her dear Prawny so truly appreciated. 'Pri-hince of my dreeeeeeams,' wailed Miss Prawn and Sugar and Spice and Pug; and, '*Do* sing it once again,' begged Pam: and just couldn't stop herself.

The afternoon passed, the sun was going down; soon there wouldn't be a minute left to go out and play. But on and on sang Miss Prawn and on and on wailed the dogs and the minute it was over, up jumped a child and asked for the song again. Their ears ached, their heads were dizzy with the noise; but on and on it went. However, now they had all been through it and come right down to the Baby. Surely this must be the end? But some old, faint memory told them that it needn't be. Nurse Matilda was quite capable of banging with her stick and starting the whole thing round again. And then round *again* . . .

The Baby stood up. Miss Prawn said, tenderly: 'Prawny sing again for Baby?'

The Baby's round face was very pink, its round blue eyes full of tears. It looked over to where Nurse Matilda stood and said, biting on a trembling lower lip: 'Nurk Magiggy?'

And Nurse Matilda put out her hand to it and suddenly it seemed to the children that her eyes were just a teeny bit less boot-buttony and her nose just a teeny bit less like two potatoes; and all about her was the faintest possible little golden glow. And she said: 'Yes, Baby?'

And the Baby looked over to where Miss Prawn stood exhausted, half proud and yet half hurt and bewildered; and said, 'Poor Prawny!'

And all the children said: 'Yes. It wasn't very nice of us really. We're sorry.'

And Nurse Matilda banged very softly with her big black stick and suddenly . . . Suddenly the sun was shining as though it were only just after teatime, and the children found themselves running gaily down the stairs and out into the garden. 'I do hope,' said Miss Prawn, following

them, hand in hand with Evangeline, 'that they
enjoyed my song.'

'Oh, I'm sure they loved it,' said Evangeline.
'You ought to have given them an encore.'

Chapter 3

HEN Nurse Matilda came down to breakfast next morning, this is what the children were doing:

Nicholas was touching up Evangeline's chocolate-brown walls with a charming design in porridge.

Christianna had borrowed a needle from the famous work-box and was secretly sewing Evangeline's sleeves to her skirt.

And all the children had taken clothes from Evangeline's wardrobe, and dressed themselves up in them.

Nurse Matilda sat down quietly at the table and said: 'Everyone eat up your porridge.'

'There isn't any porridge,' said the children, looking into the empty bowl.

Nurse Matilda pointed to the pattern of porridge thickly plastered over the walls. 'There is porridge for all,' she said.

The children turned round to the wall and began to try to lick off the porridge. It had got very cold by now and formed into unattractive lumps. By the time it was all gone their faces were quite stiff with porridge, and a rather dreadful grey, and poor Miss Prawn, entering, all eager for a glad new day, gave a shriek of horror and turned and ran out of the room. 'Miss Prawn, Miss Prawn!' cried Evangeline and tried to run after her; but her mouth was gummed up with porridge and when she lifted her arms her skirts

came too and flapped like the wings of a bat and Miss Prawn only ran faster, haring off down the dark brown corridors shrieking in a piercing voice for help. Evangeline rushed to the door after her and flung out her arms, beseeching her dear Prawny to wait. But of course her sewn-on skirts came up with them again and a swirl of draught sent her sailing off down the corridor like a sand-yacht, and out of sight.

Nurse Matilda banged once on the floor with her big black stick. 'This is the time for Evangeline's Daily Dose,' she said. A very uneasy feeling began to come over the children; some faraway memory told them that when Nurse Matilda banged with her big black stick, you had to go on with whatever you were doing. What if they had to go on wearing Evangeline's clothes (hideous dresses of turkey-red, or purple, with brown Holland overalls and button-boots – the boys were beginning to feel awful fools already) and being treated as though they *were* Evangeline?

And sure enough, they were: for they found themselves lining up and opening their mouths to receive the medicine, one by one. It was horrible medicine: a dingy grey powder, each dose weighed out into a little folded white paper package; but Nurse Matilda relentlessly marshalled each child before her, opened a packet, gave it a tap to loosen the powder, and shook it on to the out-poked tongue. Even the poor Baby, raising its blue eyes imploringly as it stood with its little beak upraised, got a dose. But I'm not sure that it got quite as much as everyone else.

A dreadful hullabaloo from outside drew them to the schoolroom windows. Miss Prawn had reached the garden by now and was fleeing along the neat, sanded paths pursued by a huge navy-blue bat which flapped its wings dreadfully as it ran, uttering muffled cries which sounded like 'Woof! Woof! Woof!' The cries were really only Evangeline, still gummed-up with porridge, calling out to Miss Prawn to stop. But Miss Prawn never paused to look behind her. Across the close-shaven green lawns she sped, leaping with thin, black-stockinged legs over borders and bushes, and after her pounded and bounded Evangeline; and after Evangeline flew Sugar and Spice, and after Sugar and Spice flew Pug, all three yelping, 'Woof! Woof! Woof!' They too had

been at the porridge – but their voices sounded like woof-woof anyway. It didn't make Miss Prawn any happier, all the same.

The children looked with some horror upon this scene; but it was nothing to their horror when a bright voice behind them cried: '*Bonjour, mes enfants*. Now – ze lesson *Française!*' and they realized that their fears were coming all too true. They had dressed themselves up in Evangeline's clothes and now they were going to have Evangeline's French lesson.

And they knew that Evangeline had also been promised by Great-Aunt Adelaide:

Private tuition in
    elocution,
    deportment,
    German,

Italian, and, above all, the pianoforte.

Oh, *dear!*

However, there was nothing to be done about it, so they collected dutifully round the square central table, covered with its red baize cloth. 'Must *we* have French, Mademoiselle?'

'*Oui, oui,*' said Mademoiselle.

Well, of course that just means 'yes' in French; but it did sound like something else and once the idea had been put into the Baby's head, it held up its hand and said, 'Eck peag.' And it seemed quite a good time-wasting idea, so all the children held up their hands too and, not waiting for permission, dashed off out of the room.

It was a long way away, down some very twisty corridors and rather hard to find, and then they had to file up and take turns; so it was quite a while before they got back, and Mademoiselle was cross. 'Have you not been too long time?' she said, in rather slow English – and added in very quick French, '*Oui, oui?*'

'But we just have,' said the children, looking puzzled. Then they thought they understood. 'Oh, you mean *you?*' they said. 'And all this time we've kept you waiting!' And taking her by the arms, with the very best intentions in the world they kindly led her off to show her the way.

Of course it wasn't what Mademoiselle had meant at all, but with so many children leading and pushing and pulling her, she could put up very little resistance. '*Laissez moi!*' she cried angrily, and, '*Je ne veux pas! Tais toi!*' But the children couldn't speak French so they only thought she was in a terrible hurry and beseeching them to be quick, and they pushed and pulled even more in their eagerness to get her there in time. Mademoiselle fought and struggled and the more she fought and struggled the more they thought she was in agonies and pushed and pulled her along. But as it was so far and they weren't too sure of the way themselves, they missed it; and soon a little mob had formed, scurrying up and down the twisting corridors with the wretched Mademoiselle in their midst, like a column of ants pushing some large edible object towards the ant-hill: with cries of, 'It's there!' 'No, it isn't – it's that way!' 'No, no, it's round this corner, I'm sure it is . . .' '*Laissez moi!*' protested Mademoiselle, marched to and fro, turned right about and marched back again, run

every which way by the children, practically lifted into the air by their kindly hands, with her feet whizzing uselessly under her like the wheels of a clockwork engine picked up off its rails . . . '*Arretez! Laissez moi!* Poot me down!' They did put her down at last, outside the door, and, feeling very proud and helpful, left her there and found their way back to the school-room. 'Poor thing!' they said to one another. 'She *was* in a state!'

Mademoiselle was still in a state when she got back. 'Verry well! I go now at vonce to your Tante Adelaide. I tell heem you have bee-have deez-grace-fool. I geeve my noteeze. I quveet.'

169

She picked up a red velvet bonnet with green velvet streamers and, clapping it back to front on her head in her agitation, marched out of the room: somewhat blinded by the ribbons which hung down in front of her furious face like a rather ragged grass mat.

So from now on, Evangeline might be having private tuition in:

Elocution,

deportment,

German,

Italian, and, above all, the pianoforte. But she would be having no French.

Out in the garden, Miss Prawn had taken refuge behind a little summer-house and crouched there, cowering, while Evangeline prowled about, waving her bat-wings and, in unison with the three dogs, still crying encouragingly through the porridge, 'Woof, woof, woof!'

The tutor who gave Evangeline her German lessons was a kind, stout old gentleman with a huge black beard, called Professor Schnorr – a very good name for him as he was always going to sleep and schnorring like anything. He led the children out into the garden, sat them down in a ring under a little willow tree on the lawn, with German grammars in their hands, sat down himself in a creaky basket-work chair, and without any more fuss went straight to sleep.

The children put down the grammars and watched him thoughtfully. Goodness, he did look hot! Already his poor bald head was becoming quite speckled with pink, as the willow moved its green arms in the breeze and let the sunbeams through. If only he had as much hair on his head as he had on his chin . . .!

'There are some scissors in Evangeline's work-box,' said Caro, thoughtfully.

'And some glue in her writing-desk,' said Lindy.

It was a bit hard to get at the back of his head, but soon Professor Schnorr had a big black beard no longer; but he did have a splendid curly black fringe. As the rest of his head was as bald as an egg, it must be confessed that he looked extremely odd.

And at that moment, several things happened.

Miss Prawn, who had finally been flushed out from behind the summer-house, came scudding round the corner with Evangeline and the three dogs in full cry; from the front door, Mademoiselle (who all this time had been having a lovely time giving in her notice) appeared with a much-enraged Great-Aunt Adelaide; and, standing quietly by a rose bed where nobody had observed her till this moment, the children saw – Nurse Matilda.

At sight of Herr Schnorr, leaping to his feet and tearing out fistfuls of black hair where, up to now, no hair at all had been, Miss Prawn came to a

skidding stop, digging her heels into the gravel so that it flew up into sharp little spurts all around her ankles, Mademoiselle cried out, 'Ooh, *la la!*' and peered with amazement through the green ribbons of her bonnet and Aunt Adelaide advanced down the steps with a look that clearly said, 'This is the end!' Sugar and Spice took advantage of the moment when everyone's attention was elsewhere, to nip Pug smartly in the behind; and Nurse Matilda raised her big black stick.

Down came the stick with a thump and Joanna picked up the scissors and walked over to Sarah and chop, chop, chop, cut off every one of Sarah's curls. 'Ow!' protested Sarah. 'Don't!' But Joanna did; she didn't want to, but somehow she couldn't help it. And before Sarah could cry 'Ow!' again, Sophie had taken the paste-brush and sloshed a little glue on to Sarah's chin; and Hetty had picked up the cut-off curls – and Sarah had a little golden beard. And Sarah had snatched the scissors from Joanna and got to work on Dominic; and Fenella was busy with the paste-pot . . . By the time they came to the Baby, every child was nearly as bald as Professor Schnorr; and every child had a beard. Considering that they were still wearing Evangeline's red and purple dressed and black button-boots, they looked very odd indeed. but snip-snip-snip went the scissors; and slosh-slosh-slosh went the paste: they didn't want to – but they couldn't stop. And now they had come to the Baby.

They stood in a miserable ring and looked at the Baby and the Baby looked back at them, woefully; but the scissors were in Rebecca's hand now and without her even moving her fingers, they seemed to be going snip, snip, snip! 'Stop, stop!' cried everyone, even the children themselves. 'Don't cut the Baby's hair!' 'Nock cucking my hairg!' cried the poor Baby, covering its curly head with two starfish hands. But Rebecca didn't stop. She couldn't stop. Snip, snip, snip went the scissors – she just couldn't help it.

The Baby took one step backward and started to run. Tripping and stumbling over Evangeline's long skirts, it ran. Her boots were far too big for it, of course, and every time it took a step they slewed round and the poor little thing, to its great astonishment, found itself staggering off in quite a different direction. But still it ran: and, staggering and tumbling, tacked across the lawn towards the rose bed and found Nurse Matilda standing there quietly with her big black stick in her hand: and clasped her round her rusty black-skirted knees. 'Nurk Magiggy,' sobbed the Baby. 'Nock wonk my hair cuck!' And it turned and looked round at the children and cried out: 'Kay peag!'

'Please,' cried the children. '*Please*, Nurse Matilda!'

Nurse Matilda stood with the Baby's hand in hers; and – yes! yes! – round her there came that little golden glow; and just for a moment she did look just a little bit less brown and wrinkly, a little bit less boot-button-eyed; a little bit less – well, ugly. And she lifted up her big black stick and gave one thump with it on the grass. And all of a sudden . . .

All of a sudden they were standing there in a ring round Professor Schnorr's creaky basketwork chair; wearing their own clothes and with their own heads of hair, straight or curly, dark or fair – and not a beard amongst them! And Herr Schnorr was as bald as ever he had been. And Miss Prawn and Evangeline were standing quietly by, and Mademoiselle's bonnet was on the right

way round and she no longer peered out through
a seaweed of green ribbons. And Nurse Matilda
was beside the rose bed with the Baby's hand in
hers; and still all about her was that golden
radiance.

And Great-Aunt Adelaide Stitch . . .

Great-Aunt Adelaide came graciously down the
front door steps towards them. 'Well, children! It
appears that you have behaved yourselves today in
model fashion. While Evangeline worked quietly
with Miss Prawn in the summer-house, the rest, it
seems, were exceedingly helpful to Mademoiselle
in a matter of some – urgency; and have spent a
useful morning under the willow tree with the

Herr Professor. I am exceedingly – gratified,' said Great-Aunt Adelaide, though for a moment it did seem as though she might be going to say 'surprised'. She added: 'As a reward, Nurse Matilda shall take you this afternoon for a visit to Madame Tussaud's Waxworks Show.'

The golden glow round Nurse Matilda suddenly went out.

Chapter 4

S O that afternoon a long line of four-wheeler cabs drew up outside Great-Aunt Adelaide's gate and the children walked down the short drive and all squashed in, the Big Ones with the Middlings perched on their knees, the Middling Ones clasping Little Ones on theirs, and some of the Little Ones even holding Tinies, so that they were piled up in castles of four to a seat. The Littlest Baby and the Littler-Baby-Still had naturally been left at home; but the Baby was there all right, having the time of its life, with its nappies looking as usual as though they were just about to come down: but never quite doing it.

Clip-clop went the sound of the horses' hooves through the London streets and there was a lovely smell of horse, and leather harness and leather-inside-of-cab. The children's heads poked out of the windows like bunches of pleased flowers and the people passing in the horse-drawn omnibuses smiled and waved back at them as they clip-clopped by. The ladies walking along the pavements looked like swans in their long dresses, all billowy with lace ruffles in front, and swirly and bustly at the back, with their big feather hats set forward on their proud heads, their hair piled up high beneath the hats. The gentlemen carried umbrellas, tightly furled; and looked rather like umbrellas themselves in their tight, dark, buttoned-up jackets. But they were all very jolly, it was such a lovely, sunshiny day; and the ladies, also, waved to the children with their gloved hands and the gentlemen flourished their curly bowler hats and it was all very gay.

At last they were at Madame Tussaud's and stood in a long restless line while Nurse Matilda and Miss Prawn counted heads and paid their entrance fees; and then they all rushed in. An Attendant, magnificent in a frogged uniform, stood at the bottom of the grand stairway, smiling helpfully; and Miss Prawn, leaving Nurse Matilda with the Little Ones and the Tinies, beneath a potted palm, tripped over to ask him directions.

The children were up the stairs the moment her back was turned, and shooting down the polished banisters, to the great astonishment of Miss Prawn who, every time she stepped forward to speak to the Attendant, found a child suddenly arriving, apparently out of heaven, between them. She turned away to look for Nurse Matilda; and at that moment Susannah took a corner of the banister too fast and landed slap on top of the Attendant. And what do you think? – the Attendant's head came right off and rolled on the

ground – still smiling politely, however, and with every sign of wishing to do anything he could to help.

'Quick – make a ring round me,' said Sebastian.

So a sort of wall of children formed itself round Sebastian, and when it dissolved there was once again a uniformed figure at the bottom of the stairs, wearing a helpful smile; only of course now it was really Sebastian and not a waxwork at all. Miss Prawn pushed her way back to him. 'Would you direct me please to the History section?' (Even a treat had to be turned by Miss Prawn into lessons; however, you couldn't blame her, with her dear pupil Evangeline lolloping up and down with joy and crying, 'Oh, good! History!')

'History!' groaned the children, turning anxious eyes upon the Attendant. The Attendant said nothing but rolled his eyes towards his left hand which was pointing downwards.

'Down there,' cried the children to Miss Prawn. 'Look, he's pointing down there.'

'Down there' turned out to be the Chamber of Horrors and they all came up again in one minute flat, driven by a pea-green Miss Prawn. 'I said the *History*,' panted Miss Prawn.

As a matter of fact, the History part of the Exhibition would have been lovely if only Miss Prawn had not been quite so keen on imparting information, and her dear pupil Evangeline on airing what she already knew. By the time they came to the Execution of Mary Queen of Scots, the children would very readily have had Evangeline's head upon the block instead of the Queen's.

Poor Mary Queen of Scots, as some children will know, lived – oh, two or three hundred years ago. She thought she ought to be Queen of England too, so Elizabeth, who really *was* Queen of England, had her head chopped off: in those days, this was the great thing to do. So there she knelt, in her black velvet dress, surrounded by nobles and ministers, and there stood the Executioner with his great big axe. 'Wouldn't it be awful if her head really was chopped off, now, here, in front of us?' said Arabella; and Romilly, just to tease Evangeline, said: 'I do believe the Executioner moved.'

'He didn't?' said Evangeline, going pale. 'Yes, he did,' said the children, playing up to Romilly; but at that moment they also went rather pale. For all

of a sudden – the Executioner did move. Up, up, up went the great axe, and very slowly down, down, down it came . . .

For Mary Queen of Scots was not a wax-work at all. It was that wicked Vicky, who had rushed on ahead with Simon and Matthew and Pam and Christopher (when there were so many children, nobody missed three or four at a time). Simon was the Executioner and the others were the nobles and ministers. And down, down, down came the axe – and round a corner came Nurse Matilda with the Little Ones all about her, like a black mother duck with her brood of restless ducklings; and she took one look and she lifted up her big black stick . . .

'Here, hey!' cried Vicky a bit anxiously, screwing round her head to look up at the slowly, slowly descending axe; and, 'Look *out*, Simon!' yelled the children, and 'Ow, ow, ow!' squealed Evangeline, darting round to hide behind Miss Prawn. But on and on, down came the axe. 'Simon, stop it!' screamed the children. But he couldn't stop it. 'Nurse Matilda,' he said, very white and scared, looking over the children's heads to where she stood, *'please!'*

Nurse Matilda looked back at him across the upturned, anxious faces, all turned to look at her now; and she bit on her lip as though – well, honestly, it looked as though she were trying to keep back a smile. And she tapped gently, once, with her stick.

And down came the axe and off flew the Queen's head and landed with a bonk on the floor. But – it wasn't Vicky's head at all: it was a wax head and the ministers and nobles and the Executioner and the Queen herself found themselves back among the rest of the children, placidly looking on. And Miss Prawn was saying, 'Well, now, shall we proceed?' as though nothing had happened.

Nurse Matilda drew near them, her brood of babies around her, all quite unconscious of what had been going on. 'I think, Miss Prawn, that Simon and Victoria are looking a little unwell. Perhaps they had better go down to the hall and sit quietly and wait for us there. Matthew and Pamela and Christopher will go with them. It is a pity they should miss the rest of the treat, but I think they quite understand why.'

Evangeline's mud-colour had by now settled down to her usual rather unlovely pink. Clinging to dear Prawny's hand, she skipped along beside her. 'Now we're coming to the Tiger Hunt, Miss Prawn. Shall I tell about tigers? The tiger is found in the continent of Asia . . .' So eager were they that neither of them noticed three figures slipping along ahead of them . . .

But Nurse Matilda did. 'Antony, Francesca and Teresa will stop handing out rifles this *minute*, please; and come down out of that elephant howdah and join those waiting in the hall . . .'

Down in the hall, Simon, Vicky and the others were having not too boring a time after all. The Attendant was still smiling helpfully at the bottom of the stairs, giving directions to anyone who cared to ask him. Healthy pink faces kept disappearing down below, only to appear looking very unhealthy indeed, protesting that they had asked for Famous Persons or The Tiger Hunt. Elderly lady visitors, demanding to know where they might leave their parasols, were directed to pompous gentlemen visitors, who were enraged to find umbrellas and sixpences pushed into their unwilling hands. A small, stout woman was pointed out to those inquiring for the figure of Queen Victoria, and found herself encircled by a gooping crowd, most of them exclaiming, 'I had no idea she was so ugly!' I can't think *who* had exchanged the two notices saying LADIES and GENTLEMEN.

'It's much more fun down here,' said Matthew and Pam, making room on the bench as they were joined by Antony and Francesca and Teresa. And gosh! they added, here were Joanna and Sarah and Rebecca and Tim. 'You can't think what we found on the way down!' said Sarah. 'A room full of . . .' Even the smiling Attendant came over to hear what they were whispering about.

By the time the visit to Madame Tussaud's Waxworks Show was over, only Miss Prawn and

Evangeline were left up in the galleries, skipping
from exhibit to exhibit with squeals of interest
and delight; and Nurse Matilda with her brood of
baby ducklings, quacking with wonder. In threes
and fours, all the rest of the children had been
banished to the hall.

But if the children were in the hall – nobody
else was. There wasn't even an attendant in sight.
Only a horde of children . . .

But what children! Some of them had two
heads: some of them had three arms: some of

them had as many as six legs, plus their arms and were crawling about among the potted palms, like centipedes; some of them had two or three feet to each leg and were leaping about like frogs. But there wasn't one child that just had one head and two arms and two legs like anybody else.

What Joanna and Sarah and Rebecca and Tim had found on their way down from the gallery was a door; and as the door was marked PRIVATE they had naturally pushed it open and gone through. And what had been behind the door was the room where all the wax heads and legs and arms were kept, for the making and mending of the waxwork figures.

No wonder the hall had so quickly emptied itself!

Miss Prawn took one look at the extraordinary assembly before her, threw up her hands, chilblains and all, and fainted dead away. She landed on top of Evangeline, who, finding herself pinned down by dear Prawny's thin legs and arms, in her bewilderment didn't realize what had happened and thought that she herself had suddenly sprouted extra limbs. With a howl of terror she struggled up and streaked out into the

Marylebone Road, as fast as she could go; and after her went the children in a forest of moving arms and legs. 'Ow, ow, ooooooow!' hooted Evangeline, scudding along the pavements in her black button-boots; and, 'Stop thief!' yelled the naughty children, pounding after her. A policeman, upon hearing this cry, stepped out with upraised hand in Evangeline's path, blowing shrilly on his whistle as he did so. All the dogs in the neighbourhood heard the whistle and came hurrying to see if there was anything going of interest to dogs: towing behind them their reluctant masters and mistresses. Soon Evangeline was surrounded by a dense crowd, insisting upon her being taken into custody at once and deported for life. 'But I haven't stolen *any*thing,' protested Evangeline. 'Look, I've got nothing in my hands. Not in any of them. Oh,' she added, looking down and counting, 'I've only got two now!'

'How many do you usually have?' asked the policeman, coldly.

'Well, I had four a few minutes ago,' said Evangeline.

The crowd immediately changed its mind and

consigned Evangeline to a padded cell instead of the hulks. 'But I did have,' she insisted. 'We all have. The other children have too. Look behind you.'

The crowd turned and looked behind itself. The children, not able to get near Evangeline and rescue her from the dreadful plight they had brought upon her, had been leaping up and down on the outside of the mob, waving their innumerable arms and begging to be heard. At sight of them, the policeman went the colour of dough, flung down his whistle and himself stampeded off down the road, the dogs following,

delighted, towing their owners – all yelling 'Ow, ow, ow!' as loudly as Evangeline herself. And a cab appeared suddenly with Nurse Matilda in it, supporting a tottering Miss Prawn, and whipped up Evangeline and sped on; and there was nothing for the children to do but to start walking home.

You'd think that with all those extra legs it would be easy: but it wasn't. Every time they put a foot down, another foot got in its way and tripped them up; besides, some of the legs were different lengths from their own – the children who had got hold of grown-up legs had to solve it by walking with two on the pavement and one in the gutter, which at least kind of evened out. By the time they arrived at Aunt Adelaide's, they were very hot, weary and hungry children indeed.

But there was no relief even now. *You* just try sitting down when you have two or three extra legs sprouting out of you – there simply isn't room! And when they stretched out their hands for their mugs, the other hands didn't seem to work the same way, but took the mugs and put them back again. And when they reached for bread and butter, one arm was too long and one was too short and neither ever seemed the right length. 'Take your arm out of the way,' they began saying crossly to one another; but they weren't their arms, they were Madame Tussaud's waxwork arms, and Madame Tussaud's arms wouldn't do what the children told them. Soon they were all fiercely squabbling and the noise of all those extra mouths quarrelling had to be heard to be believed . . .

And now the worst thing of all happened. Evangeline, whom they had been laughing at all the afternoon, had appeared in the doorway and was standing there laughing at *them*!

She laughed and she laughed. Her fat cheeks bulged with it, her eyes streamed with tears of delight at their discomfiture. 'All those legs and arms!' squealed Evangeline. 'And how hot and tired and cross you look!'

'Well, all right, Evangeline,' said the children, resentfully. 'We're sorry. We did try to stop them from deporting you for life or sending you to a lunatic asylum, but the crowd wouldn't let us get near you. We were only teasing.'

'Well, now *you're* being teased, aren't you?' said

Sebastian (Sam Honywood)

Nanny McPhee (Emma Thompson) silhouetted

Mr Brown (Colin Firth) with Baby Agatha (Hebe and Zinnia Barnes)

Mr Brown and Nanny McPhee

Mr Brown

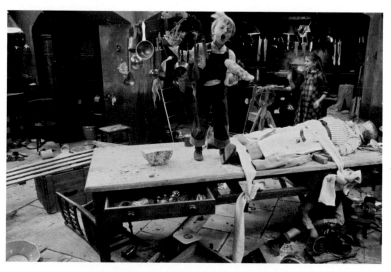

Sebastian and Christianna (Holly Gibbs)

Sebastian and Nanny McPhee

Nanny McPhee

Nanny McPhee

Aunt Adelaide (Angela Lansbury)

Aunt Adelaide

Mr Brown with his children Eric (Raphael Coleman), Tora (Eliza Bennett), Simon (Thomas Sangster), Baby Agatha (held by Nanny McPhee) [back]; Christianna, Sebastian and Lily (Jenny Daykin) [front]

Mr Brown and Aunt Adelaide

Nanny McPhee

Aunt Adelaide

Evangeline. 'And you jolly well deserve it.' And she began to jump up and down with her arms held out from her sides like a gorilla, chanting, 'La la four legs! La la two heads!' in a very silly and offensive voice.

But . . . It was a funny thing: was there or was there not growing behind Evangeline a sort of – radiance? 'Evangeline,' said the children, 'why are you – well, kind of shining?'

'Am I?' said Evangeline, surprised. But she looked round, over her shoulder. 'Oh,' she said. 'It isn't me. It's Nurse Matilda.'

'What are you doing here, Evangeline?' said Nurse Matilda.

'Teasing the children,' said Evangeline. 'Don't they look silly?'

'Yes, they do,' said Nurse Matilda. 'But they also look very miserable.'

'Well, it serves them right for being beastly to me,' said Evangeline, and began capering up and down again.

'Once people have said sorry,' said Nurse Matilda, 'that is the end of it.'

'Not with me, it isn't,' said Evangeline. 'I expect I shall go on doing this for *hours*.'

'I dare say you will,' said Nurse Matilda, very quietly; and she banged twice with her big black stick.

I don't know how long Evangeline had to go on leaping up and down, chanting, 'La la – four legs!' but certainly the children heard her still at it

as, bathed and nightgowned, teeth cleaned, prayers said and tucked into their beds at last, each with their own two arms and no more, and their own two legs and no more – they laid their heads (one apiece) on their pillows and went off to sleep.

Those extra heads and legs and arms must have got back somehow to Madame Tussaud's. I suppose Nurse Matilda saw to that.

Chapter 5

S O the days went by. There was lots to do in London, afterall, and on the whole the children were busy and happy and therefore reasonably good – if only because they were getting a bit wary about Nurse Matilda banging with her big black stick and making them go on being naughty. They went out into the park, walking two by two in a long crocodile (kept tidy by the wretched Prawn, who had to keep scudding up and down poking them back into place with her parasol) and to the exhibition at the Crystal Palace – they might have had a good time there, keeping very still and pretending to be statues, but most of the statues had nothing on and they weren't prepared to go as far as that. And they went to the Tower and pretended to Evangeline that they were going to feed Pug to the ravens, and to Kew Gardens where they abandoned her in a hot-house and she ran round and round searching for them, scarlet in the face and with perspiration breaking out all over her. And at Hampton Court they lured poor Prawn into the maze and then just kept terribly quiet so

that she thought they had all got out and left her there: and ran about like a very thin hen, distractedly clucking at the top of its voice for its chicks. And they went to the Penny Bazaar in Soho Square, and I'm sure you will all be very glad to know that what they did there, was to put all their pennies together and buy a present for Miss Prawn. It was a pink satin handkerchief-sachet with 'pen-painting' on it: a very lumpy pattern of forget-me-nots, done with oil paint splodged on with a nib. I think Miss Prawn would probably have remembered the children's visit anyway, without the aid of forget-me-nots; but she had received so little kindness in her rather bleak life that she was quite overwhelmed by the gift and, blinded by tears of emotion, banged into a door-post and had to be led home and put to bed. So perhaps it would have been better if they hadn't given it to her after all.

And then there were the lessons. Thanks to Nurse Matilda, Herr Schnorr and Mademoiselle appeared to have forgotten all about their earlier meetings; and they now plied the children with German and French; Signora Cabbargio (rightly so called, because that is exactly what she looked like) plied them with Italian, and Mr Smink, who gave Evangeline lessons in deportment and elocution, plied them with deportment and elocution. They had to watch first while Evangeline paraded the room with a board tied to her back: it seemed to serve no useful purpose but certainly made her look the most extra-ordinary shape. However, it wasn't so funny when they had to do it themselves; and then they formed into a ring and had to skip round pretending to be elves and fairies. This was mercifully interrupted by a footman arriving, chalk-white, with a message from Great-Aunt Adelaide that the house was to be abandoned at once and everyone to take to the open spaces, as England had evidently been visited, for the first time in history, by an earthquake. She herself was found hours later, flat on her face in a field. The children really felt very sorry when they saw how shaky she looked, and a bit crestfallen too, at finding London still in one piece; and wished they had given *her* the pink handkerchief-sachet. However, they had no money left. 'We could do a concert for her,' suggested Stephanie.

'Ooh, yes!' cried Evangeline, skipping with joy and nearly bringing on an earthquake all of her own. 'And I could do my recitation.'

The children were not too keen about Evangeline's recitation – they had heard it a good many times already. It was a poem of great power and beauty which she had actually made up herself, about a little girl who steals jam from the larder and causes her dear Mama to shed a tear. But so hard-hearted and lost to virtue is the little girl that the tear dries up, and for the rest of her life she seems to be wandering around looking for this wasted tear of her dear Mama's. Evangeline really let herself go on the last bit when she had grown into quite an old woman, still doddering about with an imaginary stick, looking for the tear; and finally expiring, worn out and dejected, with a loud thump on the schoolroom floor, to the great admiration of Mr Smink her elocution teacher and the great relief of everyone else.

However, if Evangeline could make up poems so could they, and there was a great deal of muffled squeaking and giggling in corners as they thought up some contributions of their own. Miss Prawn would be having her evening off and was taking Nurse Matilda to visit her Mama. Her Mama was in fact a horrid old thing who took all Miss Prawn's meagre earnings and spent them on cheese, of which she was inordinately fond. Miss Prawn, however, was devoted to her and dashed round at every spare moment with even more presents of cheese. But it meant that fortunately nobody would be there who would really *hear* the poems. 'We can arrange something about Aunt Adelaide's ear trumpet,' said the children.

So that evening after supper they all trooped down to the drawing-room, where Aunt Adelaide was sitting in a chair of state, with Parrot in his cage on one side of her and Canary on the other, and Pug at her feet; all quite excited at the treat in store.

Of course Evangeline went first. Arrayed in one of the turkey-red dresses, with yellow blodges all over it this time, she stood up, as taught in Mr Smink's deportment lessons, shoulders well back – which unfortunately meant stomach well out – hands hanging limply at her sides like small underdone suet puddings. Aunt Adelaide clapped her own horny hands together, Parrot screeched 'Anchors aweigh!' which was all this very dull bird could say. Evangeline dipped a curtsy, one foot crumpling uncomfortably behind her, and announced: 'THE LOST TEAR.'

'What, dear? Can't hear,' said Aunt Adelaide,

leaning forward like a one-horned cow, the trumpet stuck in her ear.

'THE LOST TEAR,' bellowed Evangeline, and began.

'Oh, list to me while I do tell
What to a girl called Maria befell.
It is a tale I fear most sad
Because Maria turned out bad.'

'Bravo, bravo!' cried Great-Aunt Adelaide, waving the ear trumpet, apparently under the impression that this was the end. It by no means was, but she was delighted to discover it. She was not of a literary turn herself and could not get over Evangeline having made it up. Standing behind her chair, Mr Smink gestured encouragement. Evangeline continued.

'This girl her happiness did sell
Because her mother made some jell-
Y and did leave it on the shelf.
She did not say, "Help yourself."
'But Maria to that shelf did come.
At first she took only some.
But soon there was no longer plenty
For the pot of jam was empty.'

Behind Great-Aunt Adelaide, Mr Smink peered into an imaginary pot, living again the part of Mama at the moment of discovery. Evangeline also lifted hands in horror and put on a dreadfully long face.

' "Alas, where did that jelly go,
My dear Maria, do you know?"
Oh, listeners! – what must I relate?
I do not like to say it quite.
' "Speak out! To your Mama reply!"
Listeners! – Maria told a lie.
A lie she told Mama I fear.
Her poor Mama did shed a tear . . .'

And so they had come at last to the lost tear

and after about eleven more verses Evangeline (and Mr Smink) had grown old and feeble, doddering about gooping into pretence corners, looking for the wasted tear; and they were able to rush forward and raise the large lump of Evangeline where she lay expiring on the floor, and with many bows share Aunt Adelaide's loud applause. Agatha seized the opportunity to remove a piece of toffee from her gums where she had been nursing it all this time, and stuff it as far as it would go down Aunt Adelaide's ear trumpet.

Mr Smink departed, exhausted, and the next part of the concert began. Jennifer – rather terrified now that they had really got to the point – stood up and gabbled off a poem she had made up about Great-Aunt Adelaide herself –

'Great-Aunt Adelaide, she bought a woolly coat,
She grew a little beard and she thought she was a goat.
The children started laughing, they thought it was so silly,
She didn't seem to KNOW if she was a Nanny or a Billy.'

This was very well received by the children

except for Evangeline who burst into loud boo-hoo-hoos and said she would tell Aunt Adelaide. However, it was very hard to tell Aunt Adelaide anything because of the toffee in her ear trumpet. To punish Evangeline for being so sneaky, Helen leapt up and did one about Miss Prawn –

'Poor Miss Prawn's so skinny and skimpy,
When she floats in her bath she looks more like a
shrimpy.'

The children thought this was funnier than ever, especially the Little Ones who turned it into a song and hopped up and down chanting it, like a lot of miniature Red Indians; which quite drowned Evangeline's efforts to bellow into the ear trumpet that the horrid children were being disrespectful. 'I'll do one about Mr Smink,' said Louisa –

'Mr Smink, what do you think? –
When he takes off his boots his feet do –'

'Louisa!' screamed the children, divided between horror and hilarity. 'Now Gumble,' said Quentin.

So Megan did one about Gumble –

'Gumble, the butler, 'e
Sat on some cutlery;

Goodness, he did feel sore!
The knives, forks and spoons
Inflicted such wounds
That he'll never sit down no more.'

This, however, was too much for the Baby; it couldn't bear the idea of poor Gumble not being able to sit down. Rhiannon had to make up one about Fiddle, to help it forget –

'Poor old Fiddle
She danced on a griddle,
But it was dreadfully hot.
So, right in the middle,
She did a great w –'

'Rhiannon!' screamed all the children again.

'– which cooled it down a lot,' finished Rhiannon triumphantly.

This one had almost as fatal an effect, for it reduced the Baby to such a paroxysm of giggling that it had to be picked up and hugged and shaken and beaten on the back. I'm afraid Fiddle's sufferings were quite lost, in the Baby's delight in a grubby joke.

Encouraged by its ecstatic chuckling, Sally made up another one –

'Professor Schnorr, he took off his vest

But — it was rather rummy —
His beard was so huge that it covered his chest
And even a bit of his tummy —'

and this reduced it to such a state of helplessness that they had to leave it to recover and do one about Evangeline's Intended, Adolphus Haversack —

'When Adolphus was a little boy, his Ma went to the
* Zoo with him,*
She went to the Head Keeper and she asked what
* they could do with him.*
She said, "Please keep Adolphus, and I'll pay an
* honorarium,"*
But they thought she said "a dolphin" and he's
* now in the aquarium.'*

This was the end for Evangeline, who gave a great howl of rage, seized Aunt Adelaide's trumpet and began angrily hitting out with it at whatever child came nearest. A great deal of shouting and ow-ow-ow-ing ensued, Parrot joining in with raucous cries of 'Anchors aweigh!', Canary shrilling, Sugar and Spice nipping away at Pug, till all the air was filled with tufts of brown hair: ow-ow-ow-ing pretty loudly themselves as Pug nipped back. Great-Aunt Adelaide, not able to

ignore the fact that it was Evangeline who had
started the trouble and, anyway, wanting to get
her ear trumpet back, swiped out at her with the
cushion of her chair, which burst into a fine
flurry of feathers. If Aunt Adelaide could wage a
pillow-fight, so could the children, and they all
snatched up cushions and laid about them too.
Some of the feathers floated down into the ear
trumpet and got glued up with the toffee, and
soon a sort of bird's nest had formed there, into
which Canary flew and sat serenely singing. Even
Aunt Adelaide could hear the trilling, muffled
though it might be with feathers and toffee, when

she had finally wrested back the ear trumpet from Evangeline; and she thought something must have gone seriously wrong with her hearing, and began to ring the bell for someone to go and fetch the doctor. The Baby, who had decided that its own turn had come, had meanwhile climbed laboriously on to a chair and now stood there, rather mournful because nobody would listen to its party piece. The room was in pandemonium, so thick with fur and feathers and the sound of dogs barking, Canary shrilling, children laughing, Evangeline howling, Aunt Adelaide exclaiming and Parrot shrieking 'Anchors aweigh!' that nobody heard the door open; until into the bedlam Nurse Matilda's voice said: 'You rang, Madam?' and suddenly silence fell.

Great-Aunt Adelaide held out the ear trumpet. 'I have a curious singing in my ears.'

Nurse Matilda took the ear trumpet, poked down a curled forefinger and hooked out the bird's nest, Canary and all. 'Well, there! I can hear perfectly again,' said Aunt Adelaide, greatly astonished. She glanced round the room somewhat uncertainly. 'We have had a delightful entertainment, Nurse. Charming.'

'Evidently, Madam,' said Nurse Matilda; and she lifted up her big black stick.

From the chair, the Baby held out its fat hands. 'Nurk Magiggy! Nurk Magiggy!' And, pleased to have the attention of its audience at last, it made an unsteady bob curtsy. The children looked at it with love and pity. What could it possibly know, poor little thing, that it could perform?

'Kinging ge Goognike Kong,' said the Baby.

So they all stood round and sang with the Baby the song that their mother used to sing to them as she tucked them up in bed . . .

'Mama must go now,
Time for your bed now,
On your white pillow
Lay your little head now.
'The dark is a friend, so
We'll turn out the light.
Today's at an end, so
Darlings, good night!'

Great-Aunt Adelaide sat quietly, the cow's-horn of her ear trumpet bent forward to listen to the children's voices. When the singing was over, Nurse Matilda let her black stick down very gently to the floor, without any bang at all. 'Very

210

Ma - ma must go now, time for your bed now;

On your white pil-low lay your lit-tle head now.

The dark is a friend, so we'll turn out the light,

To-day's at an end, so dar - lings, good night!

well, children,' she said. 'We will now go upstairs. The Big Ones will remain to clear up, and then follow.' And she lifted up the Baby and, holding it in the crook of her arm, gave Aunt Adelaide a respectful little bob. 'Good night, Madam. Good night, Miss Evangeline.'

'Good night, Nurse,' said Great-Aunt Adelaide; and she added to Evangeline, 'An ill-favoured woman. But just this evening – didn't you think she looked somewhat less – homely?'

'And all golden-y,' said Evangeline. 'I've noticed it before.'

Chapter 6

NE day, Nurse Matilda said to the children: 'I have a message from your Great-Aunt Adelaide. Tomorrow evening, she is giving a soirée. A soirée is an evening party. Your Great-Aunt Adelaide wishes the older children to be present, in their best clothes. The rest will go to bed at the usual time.'

'Oh, no!' groaned all the children. The Big Ones didn't want to go to Aunt Adelaide's soirée (or anywhere else) in their best clothes, and the Little Ones didn't want to go to bed at the usual time.

The next morning, when the children came in from their half-hour of Healthful Fresh Air before breakfast, this is what they had been doing:

Daniel had pinned up a large notice at the Tradesmen's entrance, saying: INFECTOUIS DISEESE, NO ADMITTENS. Hannah had

mixed some of the schoolroom chalk with water and filled up all yesterday's milk-bottles with it.

Tora had painted little red spots on the glass pane of the big front door.

The other children had dug up lots of worms in case they might come in useful, at Aunt Adelaide's soirée.

Cook became more and more mystified as the morning wore on and no butcher or baker or fishmonger arrived with their goods for that evening's party. 'Drat them tradesmen!' she said to Nurse Matilda, over their elevenses in the Servants' Hall. 'And the extra help hasn't come either. But I must say, your young ladies and gentlemen are being very helpful. I never did see such children for helpfulness.'

The children were indeed being very busy assisting with preparations for Great-Aunt Adelaide's soirée.

Jaci had made a little hole in the bottom of the kettle and every time Cook put it on the range, in two minutes it was empty and the fire underneath had gone out.

Hetty was standing beside Cook as she made her sausage rolls, and as fast as Cook filled one, she prodded the sausage out and put it quietly back with

215

the rest. ('I must have mistook me quantities,' said Cook, looking with dismay at the undiminished pile of sausages still waiting to be wrapped round with pastry.)

Sophie was curling the worms up lovingly on the little chocolate cakes.

Justin had opened the sandwiches and was putting in a teeny thin layer of wet cotton wool; and closing them up again.

Toni had filled up the coffee tin with earth.

Arabella had wrapped a crêpe bandage round the fruit cake and covered the whole thing with icing.

Clarissa had folded a yellow duster in with the sponge roll and Cook was quite happy, thinking it was apricot jam.

Agatha had sewn together the knees of Gumble's best evening trousers, and the hem of Fiddle (the parlourmaid's) dress.

Sebastian had filled the toes of their shoes with a stiff greengage jelly.

All the other children were helping with Great-Aunt Adelaide's party too.

And that afternoon, by great good fortune, as they were playing about in the garden, who should arrive but Signora Cabbargio, all eager for the fray. She was going to sing at the soirée, and was in a great state because she couldn't find anyone to translate her Italian song into English. The children were only too happy to help her and soon she was practising away, under the willow tree, at a song which largely consisted of the words, 'La Great-Aunt Adelaide-a, Ees a seely old fool-a . . .'

And so the evening of the party came. The younger ones were put to bed and immediately got up again and cautiously scuttled downstairs. The Big Ones resentfully climbed into their best clothes – the girls in white embroidered dresses, half-way down their calves and dreadfully scratchy with starch, the boys in white sailor suits with their trousers half-way down *their* calves. I must say they looked hideous; but Evangeline far outshone them in a dress of an incredibly nasty green with lemony squirls all over it. Great-Aunt Adelaide herself was resplendent in purple satin; with her hair – and a lot of false hair too – piled up in large lumps and blobs on top of her head, rather as though someone had been making mud-pies there and just left them. Stuck in among the mud-pies were lots of combs and feathers, and dropped in among the feathers by Susie, although Aunt Adelaide did not know it, were some monkey nuts. Parrot was very fond of monkey nuts.

Aunt Adelaide also did not know that behind every chair and curtain and under every table, were hidden small and middling children, already in the last stages of muffled giggling.

Gumble and Fiddle had been given a light snack by Cook before the party began, as the tradesmen hadn't arrived with their proper supper. They had had a fearful time with the cotton-wool sandwiches, chewing away like goats but getting no further, and it had made them late for everything. They were still struggling into their clothes as the first bell rang, and with great shrieks of 'They're here!' and 'My feet!' and 'Drat it!' (from Cook, who had been having an anxious time too, because the decorations on her little chocolate cakes simply wouldn't stay still) – they hastened out into the hall. But what with the legs of Gumble's trousers having been stitched together at the knees, and the hem of Fiddle's skirt being sewn into a bag, it ended in a sort of sack race: all the worse because the jelly in their

shoes kept oozing out, squidge, squidge, round
their ankles as they hopped and lolloped to the
front door and peered through the glass pane at
the first arrivals.

You remember that Tora had that morning
painted the glass all over with little red spots?

The first guests were, in fact, Sir Choppup de
Lot and his Lady. Sir Choppup de Lot was a
famous foreign surgeon. He had chopped up
Aunt Adelaide's late husband right, left and
centre, and although she had immediately
become a widow, she had great faith in him. But
now . . . 'Goot heavints!' exclaimed Sir Choppup,
peering in through the glass as Gumble peered
out. 'Vot eest mit de bootlaire? He iss covet mit
spots!'

And at the same moment, Gumble cried out:
'Oh, my goodness! Sir Choppup and her
ladyship! Spots all over them!'

Fiddle was in a terrible taking. 'Measles!
Chicken-pox! Come over them sudden in the
kerridge as they was driving here!' and off she
went, hop, hop, squidge, squidge, to the drawing-
room to tell Madam: entering with a last flying
leap most upsetting to the nerves of Great-Aunt

Adelaide Stitch. 'What on earth is the matter, Fiddle? Control yourself!'

'People with spots, Madam!' gasped Fiddle, exhausted with emotion and hopping. 'Trying to get in!'

'People with spots?' cried Aunt Adelaide. 'This is not an Isolation Hospital. Drive them away!'

'Drive them away: Madam says, drive them away!' cried Fiddle, bounding back into the hall.

'Go away, go away!' echoed Gumble obediently, making violent shoo-ing gestures through the glass.

'Gone out of hiss mindt,' said Sir Choppup, quietly. 'Med! Ravink!' And he took Lady de Lot by the arm and led her down the steps again. 'Be prepart for bat newss, my dear! Be brave! Mit spots, and ravink med: I know ter signs. It iss ter Plague.'

'The Plague?' squealed Lady de Lot. A second carriage had just bowled in through the gate and she rushed to it. 'Don't stop, drive off, save yourselves! The house is stricken with the Plague!' And she leapt into her own carriage after Sir Choppup and they never stopped until they came to Dover; and there took the Ostend packet, leaving all their possessions behind, and were never heard of in England again. Wasn't it sad for them?

Gumble, meanwhile, had got the front door open and as there was now no spotted glass between them, he admitted the next lot of guests without further trouble and they were able to tell Aunt Adelaide all about the lunatics they had met, who had burbled to them about the Plague and rushed off into the night. From under the tables and behind the sofas and chairs, the children listened and nearly split themselves with laughing.

By ten o'clock most of the guests had arrived, graciously received by Great-Aunt Adelaide, complete with mud-pie hair-do, combs, feathers, Parrot and all – for Parrot had found the nuts by now and unknown to Great-Aunt Adelaide was happily scrabbling about for them on top of her head; and Gumble and Fiddle were free of the front door and able to hurry about offering trays of refreshment. The stitching had come apart and they no longer had to proceed in kangaroo hops and bounds, but the jelly oozing out of their shoes was proving a great attraction to Pug and Sugar and Spice, who followed them about devotedly. Susie had tied the loose end of a reel of black cotton to the tail of each dog. The cotton was forming a splendid web of almost invisible thread about the legs of the guests, as the dogs wove their way between them, trailing Fiddle and Gumble.

Evangeline stood smugly at Great-Aunt Adelaide's side, bobbing a curtsy to each new guest, holding her hands out, bent at the wrists, in an excessively silly and affected way. 'We'll soon put an end to *that*,' said the children; and snip, snip went a pair of scissors through the buttons and

bows at Evangeline's back and brrrrrrp! went
the elastic of Evangeline's knickers . . . 'Good
evening, Ma'am! How d'ye do, Ma'am,' piped
Evangeline, bobbing her fiftieth curtsy; and
suddenly whoops! went Evangeline's pants, down
round her ankles. She gave a stout wriggle and
surreptitiously hauled them up, but the next guest
was upon her. 'Evangeline, your curtsy!' hissed
Great-Aunt Adelaide. 'Yes, Aunt,' said Evangeline,
wretchedly bobbing – and whoops! down they
came again. All round the room, the drawn

curtains shook and bellied with the ecstasy of the Middling Ones and the Little Ones, trying to stifle their laughter.

At ten o'clock came a great moment – the arrival of Mr and Mrs Haversack and Adolphus. Adolphus was the young man chosen by Great-Aunt Adelaide to marry Evangeline when she should be old enough.

The guests had been having a rather puzzling time with the earth coffee and hollow sausage-rolls – (fortunately, perhaps, none of the little chocolate cakes would stay still long enough for anybody to eat one) – and were quite glad to stop enjoying the light refreshments and turn to watch the great entry. 'My dear Adelaide – so delighted!' cried the guests of honour, advancing upon their hostess with outstretched hands . . .

Or trying to advance: for by this time the whole room was a network of knee-high black thread, and they found themselves to their great astonishment, flung back and out in the hall again. 'Come in, my dears, come in!' begged Aunt Adelaide, surprised, trying to surge forward in her turn, to meet them. But she too was flung back with a jerk, and Parrot, dozing among the combs and feathers on her head, lost his balance and gave a shrill shriek of 'Anchors aweigh!' '*What*, dear?' cried the Haversacks, appearing in the doorway and disappearing backwards into the hall again, as the black threads caught them across their knees. Between hall and drawing-room, Gumble stood ankle-deep in greengage jelly, a look of numbed bewilderment on his face.

At the far end of the room, Signora Cabbargio had meanwhile burst into song, holding the children's translation at arm's length as she blissfully warbled away. 'La Great-Aunt Adelaide-a, Ees a seely old fool-a,' carolled Madame Cabbargio. Great-Aunt Adelaide caught her own name now and again and graciously bowed and smiled. She observed with quiet satisfaction that her guests seemed quite spellbound by the beauty of the song: standing with bent heads, staring down at their toes, purple with suppressed emotion.

Away at the door, Mr and Mrs Haversack were still beating back and forth at the web of cotton stretched across the doorway, as though thrown up on a shore and sucked back again by heavy seas. 'Come in, come in!' hooted Great-Aunt

Adelaide, high-stepping towards them over the mesh, Parrot clinging for dear life to the mud-pies, Evangeline following, clinging for dear life to the legs of her knickers. 'We can't!' cried Mr and Mrs Haversack, despairing. The guests stood gaping, torn between horror and joy. The hidden children held their aching tummies and could hardly bear to laugh any more.

Fortunately, at this moment Signora Cabbargio ended her song and, bowing right and left to the applause, barged her way like a triumphant elephant out of the room, the network smashed and trampled before her enormous progress. Her going left a pathway, through which Mr and Mrs Haversack could at last advance. Adolphus bowed and lifted Evangeline's hand to his lips. She let go for a moment: and whoops! down came one leg.

Sally, who all this time had been nursing Evangeline's canary for just the right occasion, decided that it had come. The canary gave a happy chirrup at being set free, and flew softly down and settled in Mr Haversack's beard. Everything about Mr Haversack was expensive – even his beard was golden; the canary was just the same colour and in a moment invisible.

'Evangeline,' commanded Aunt Adelaide. 'Your curtsy!'

'I can't,' mumbled Evangeline, anxiously hauling on the fallen knicker-leg. And anyway, the time was approaching for her party-piece. 'I must go,' she muttered and, giving one last desperate hitch, walking stiffly like a prisoner in leg-irons, she crept away.

'Poor child, she is unwell. Mr Haversack and I will overlook it. Will we not, my dear?' said Mrs Haversack, all gracious kindliness. But Mr Haversack himself seemed not, entirely well, for his beard began to fluff itself up in a really alarming manner and he answered only in a series of shrill little chirps. 'He has had no dinner; we were delayed,' said Mrs Haversack, looking at him anxiously. 'A crumb to eat, perhaps?' A crumb in fact would have been just the thing, or even some bird-seed; but she espied Fiddle, squelching round with a delicious-looking jam roll. 'A slice of this, perhaps? Haversack is so fond of apricot; aren't you, my dear?'

Mr Haversack burst into a prolonged chirruping, quite as astonishing to himself as to his neighbours. Mrs Haversack sawed at the

yellow duster rolled into the sponge. The children shook and sobbed with laughter, and almost longed for it to end.

The miserable Evangeline, meanwhile, had climbed up on to the small dais prepared, tightly gripping the sides of her skirts, and now announced THE LOST TEAR, and dropped a curtsy. Nothing else dropped this time as, in holding on to her dress she was also holding up her pants.

'Oh, list to me while I do tell
What to a girl called Maria befell —'
'Beautiful, beautiful!' said Mrs Haversack.

'She made it all up herself,' said Great-Aunt Adelaide, proudly.

'Prrrrrrrr-up,' said Mr Haversack's beard.

From his corner, poor Mr Smink gazed upon his pupil in despair, as the poem progressed. For where was the note of pathos which they had so devotedly rehearsed together? Where were the actions, the telling gestures? The imaginary kitchen table with Mama using both hands to make an imaginary pot of jelly . . . The high shelf, with Maria reaching up both hands to take down the imaginary pot and gollop up the lot . . . ' "Alas! —" ' prompted Mr Smink, violently signalling from his corner, throwing up both arms in horror as Mama discovers the loss of the jam; but Evangeline only turned upon him a look of anguish and, with her hands glued to her sides, ploughed on.

The children were so hysterical with laughter that the Big Ones had to creep in with the others, under the tables and chairs and behind the curtains, to hide themselves from the grown-ups . . . The younger Ones were quite sick with it already, doubled up with giggles; and under the huge centre table, the Baby was being very silly, marching up and down with its nappies trailing, rather bent because the table wasn't quite high enough, and reciting Evangeline's poem in its own language. Every now and then it collapsed in a small heap of squeaking giggles and then, encouraged by the helpless laughter of the rest, staggered up and was off again. The children rocked and rolled and burst with laughter, hugging their aching tummies, begging it to stop; but so much success had gone to its head and off it went again. After a bit, other children crawled across from other tables and chairs and sofas, and soon there was a sort of encampment under the big middle table. And then more children came and more, and the long table-cloth began to bulge and heave with so many of them being there, and all of them rolling about with laughter.

It was really extraordinary that the grown-ups didn't discover them . . .

Very extraordinary . . .

They lifted up the edge of the table-cloth and peered out between the bobbles.

There weren't any grown-ups there any more. While they had laughed and laughed, and cried with laughter – the party had ended, the guests had all gone home. 'Thank goodness,' said the children, crawling out from under the table, hugging their aching tummies, wiping their streaming eyes. 'We can stop laughing now and go up to bed . . .'

But Nurse Matilda stood in the doorway; and she lifted her big black stick and gave one bang with it on the drawing-room floor: and the children began to laugh again.

They laughed and they laughed. The tears ran down their faces and their cheeks ached and their tummies ached, but they couldn't stop it; and if they even seemed to begin to stop, one of them would say, 'Fly at once, it iss ter Plague!' and off they would go again; and if that began to dry up, another would warble, 'Seely old fool-a,' or the Baby would stagger up and start stumping up and down imitating Evangeline; or they would all start thinking about the yellow-duster jam roll. Or if they really did seem to be recovering at last, someone would cry out: 'Whoops!' and they would all fall about into paroxysms of hysteria once more.

They laughed and they laughed. They longed to stop, but they couldn't stop. They were worn out with it, exhausted with it, longing to end it; but they couldn't . . . All over the house, the lights would be going out, Evangeline, worn out with her triumphs would be fast asleep in bed, Great-Aunt Adelaide would be taking off some of the mud-pies, combing the nutshells out of the rest; Fiddle and Gumble would be shaking the last of the jelly out of their shoes . . . But *they* must laugh and laugh – aching with it, sobbing with it, rolled up against one another in an absolute agony; praying, 'Oh, let it stop! Let it stop!'

Nurse Matilda stood in the doorway and watched them. 'Oh, Nurse Matilda,' they cried, 'do let us stop!' And they said to the Baby, 'You ask her, Baby. Go to Nurse Matilda and ask her to bang with her stick again, and let us stop.'

The Baby sat in a round, doleful bundle

beneath the big table, its blue eyes brimming with tears of giggling, but longing only to go to its little bed. 'Carnk,' it said. 'Koo karg!'

'Oh, poor little thing!' cried the children. 'It's too tired.' And they picked it up and staggered with it over to Nurse Matilda. 'Please, Nurse Matilda, just let the Baby off. Never mind us, if you'll let the Baby off.'

'Ah,' said Nurse Matilda. 'That's better, isn't it?' The Baby stood rocking with weariness before her

and she stooped down and lifted it up in her arms; and in that moment it was asleep, its head on her rusty black shoulder.

And the children weren't laughing any more. They stood all around her, quietly, and she said to them – quietly – 'Sometimes what amuses us is rude and hurtful to others: isn't it?' And without another word, still carrying the sleepy Baby in her arms, she led them out into the hall and up the broad staircase and said: 'All go to bed now. And no noise, please. No giggling.'

The children went to bed. They made no noise and you can be sure there was no giggling. But they did say just a few words to one another before they went off to sleep. 'When Nurse Matilda smiles,' they said, 'just for a moment — doesn't she look pretty?'

Chapter 7

AND so the days went by and, worn out perhaps by the really enormous amount of naughtiness they had expended on Great-Aunt Adelaide's soirée, the children went quite gaily along with hardly any outbreaks. They went to the Zoo and, apart from shutting Evangeline into an empty monkey cage (to the delight of the neighbouring monkeys who kept pressing bits of bun on her, squeezing them through the bars) – and joining a crocodile of convent school-children, to the great mystification of the nuns in charge, who suddenly found themselves with twice as many pupils as they had started out with – they really behaved very well. True, they did once change Aunt Adelaide's great flowered hat back to front, and she drove through the park bowing graciously to

her friends, all unaware that she looked as though someone had sewn a packet of mixed seeds on her forehead; but she never knew, so perhaps it hardly counted? And they did label a large bar of yellow soap 'Cheese', and send it off to Miss Prawn's horrid old mother; but actually it was rather a success, so we needn't count that either. (She was so greedy that she ate her way steadily through it and by the end acquired quite a taste for it. At first Miss Prawn was much alarmed as she approached their little house, to see bubbles floating out of the dining-room window; but she soon got used to finding the old lady in a rich white lather and the soap was cheaper so I'm glad to say in the end she saved quite a lot of money.) But really one can say that they were pretty good, and Nurse Matilda took them to all sorts of interesting places and told them stories and read to them and she seemed to get prettier and more smile-y every day, and on the whole they were having a lovely time, when –

When –!

When one afternoon, Nurse Matilda came to the schoolroom and said: 'Your Great-Aunt

Adelaide is entertaining a friend to tea. Her name is Mrs Green. You are to wash your hands and faces and put on your best clothes and go down and meet her.'

'How lovely!' cried Evangeline, hastening off with Miss Prawn to choose yet another of her ghastly dresses. 'How awful!' began the children. But they took one look at the big black stick and said instead, 'Yes, Nurse Matilda,' and went down quietly as they had been told and sat down in a ring round Great-Aunt Adelaide and Mrs Green. And Mrs Green said, 'I never *saw* such well-behaved children.'

'Aren't they?' said Great-Aunt Adelaide. Their behaviour had certainly improved of late and she thought it was all due to the virtuous example set them by her dear Evangeline.

'When I left home,' said Mrs Green, 'this is what *my* children were doing:

Mary had fastened the back buttons of the Little Ones' pinafores together and they were marching about crabwise in little clumps, quite sick with giggles. Valerie had heard that eating paper makes you stammer and was feeding pages to the poodle trying to make him go w-w-woof!

Alison had hidden the budgerigar and put the cat in its cage instead; and Grandmama was having hysterics, seeing him sitting there calmly smiling at her and licking his lips.

Adam had collected the whole of the family mail and posted it in the boiler.

Cecily and William had waxed the seat of the new governess's chair and every time she sat down she shot off again, to her great amazement. And —

Marcus had put a thin layer of paint over her spectacles and the poor thing was seeing everything pink and thought she had conjunctivitis.

All my other children were doing simply dreadful things too.'

'The person you need,' said Great-Aunt Adelaide, 'is Nurse Matilda.'

A funny, funny feeling began to creep over the children, as though, long ago, all this had happened before. They said, quickly: 'Only you can't have her. She's ours.'

And Nurse Matilda stood in the doorway and she smiled — but yet, at the same time two big tears gathered in her eyes and began to roll down her cheeks. And as they rolled — they seemed to roll away with them the last of Nurse Matilda's

wrinkles; and her face wasn't round and brown
any more and her nose, like two potatoes, was
changing its shape altogether, and even her rusty
black dress seemed to be getting all golden-y. And
she said: 'Ah, children – you've forgotten how I
work! When you do need me, but don't want me
– then I must stay. But when you don't need me,
and do want me – then I have to go.'

'Oh, no!' cried the children. 'You can't!' And
they began to think up naughty things to do
immediately. It was strangely difficult, but they
did manage to think of a few. 'We still aren't *very*
good,' they said hopefully.

'But my children are worse,' pleaded Mrs Green.

'That does seem to be true,' said Nurse Matilda to the children; and she made a bob curtsy to Great-Aunt Adelaide, and said: 'With your permission, then, Ma'am, I shall start work with Mrs Green first thing tomorrow morning.' And she smiled at the children and she looked so lovely – in spite of that one huge sticking-out tooth – that they all started crying and begging, 'Don't go! Don't go!'

But that night, when they were all tucked up in bed, she came round and to every child gave a special kiss and a special hug; and said a rather special 'good night'. And when she had gone out, softly closing the door behind her, they said to each other: 'Did she say "good night"? Wasn't it really "goodbye"?' And they knew in their hearts that it had really been 'goodbye'.

Chapter 8

ERHAPS it was because their hearts were so heavy that night that the children began to dream. At least it was a sort of dream. Afterwards they were never quite sure how much of it had been a dream and how much of it was real – and all the time with that odd feeling that something very much like this had happened before.

The dream was that after Nurse Matilda had closed the doors and all the house was quiet, they got up again and crept out into the garden, and all met together under the willow tree and said: 'Well, we're jolly well not going to stay here without her. Let's go home! Let's run away.'

And all of a sudden, before they knew how it had happened, they *were* running away.

They couldn't stop it.

The house was very quiet, standing tall and gaunt and grim, resentfully watching them go; and it seemed to swing its gate wide open and say, 'All right, go on, get on with it; we don't want you here, anyway.' And they felt themselves almost pushed and hustled out, and when they looked back doubtfully at the gate and wondered whether they shouldn't, after all, go back, it swung-to again and closed itself in their faces; and they saw that there was a sign on it saying, NO RE-ADMITTENS ON ACCOUNT OF INFECTOUIS DISEESE. So anyway, they couldn't go back. They just had to go on.

They began to run. The streets were very dark and quiet, only the gas lamps throwing pools of light, splashed like gold sovereigns along the pavement's edge. The tall houses seemed to close upon them their shuttered eyes, saying disdainfully, 'You are rude and ungrateful, running away from *us*.' 'But we can't help it,' they tried to say. 'We don't really want to, we were only just thinking about it . . .' But their mouths seemed to be full of glue and it only came out M'f, m'f, m'f. And on they ran.

On they ran. Miss Prawn had appeared and

now ran with them, poking them back into line with her parasol while with the other hand she administered great mouthfuls of Evangeline's daily dose. They tried to fob her off with a pink satin handkerchief-sachet, painted with blodgy forget-me-nots, but she only cried out, 'No, no, it'll make me bang into a door-post,' and went on administering the Gregory powders. They had to redouble their speed to get away from her.

They ran and they ran. The Big Ones ran first, the Middlings trailing after them, the Littlies trailing after *them*, lugging the Tinies; the Baby last of all, stumping along on its fat bent legs, determined as usual not to be left behind. Sugar and Spice trotted gaily in the rear, full of happy memories, no doubt, of all the nips they had taken at Pug.

On and on. It was rather hard to run and when they looked down they saw that they were wearing Evangeline's button-boots and the boots were filled with Evangeline's dull, red, schoolroom-tea plum jam. And when by much jumping and shaking they managed to dislodge it, the boots were much too large for them and slewed round as they ran, sending them tacking

back and forth across the street, like a fleet of
reluctant little ships. And their clothes were
Evangeline's hideous dresses, much too small for
the Big Ones, much too big for the Littlies; and
their hats were Aunt Adelaide's great, overgrown-
garden hats, which also were much too big for
them and fell down over their eyes and half
blinded them. It didn't matter because they just
had to keep on running anyway.

And at last – help in sight! Round a corner
came cloppeting a four-wheeler cab and a lady

and gentleman got out of it and came hastening towards them crying, 'Goot heavints! Vot eest mit ter childrence? You are runnink avay?' 'Oh, Sir Choppup de Lot!' cried the children. 'Oh, Lady de Lot – please help us! We don't *want* to be running away! Please tell us the way back.' But the kindly faces turned towards them and they saw that Sir Choppup and his lady were covered in spots. 'Measles! Chicken-pox! The Plague!' shrieked the children, not able to stop themselves; and their boots took control and sent them tearing off in the opposite direction. Echoes of, 'Med! Ravink! Gone out dere mindts!' came back to them as Sir Choppup handed Lady de Lot back into the cab and turned the horse's head for Dover. 'And all mit little pearts,' said Sir Choppup, sadly. 'Like nanny-koats and pilly-koats, all mit little pearts!'

And it was true: for suddenly their chins had sprouted little golden beards and they bleated as they ran.

They ran and they ran. Between the tall houses, past the Zoo, where all the monkeys came out and pelted them with bits of bun, past Madame Tussaud's, where an Attendant stood, smiling at them helpfully. 'How can we get back to Great-Aunt Adelaide's?' called the children, streeling past him; but he only smiled helpfully on, and they saw that he had eight arms and they were all pointing in different directions.

'Oh,' cried the children, gasping and sobbing, 'if only we could stop!'

But they couldn't. The dawn came, palely creeping up over the roofs of London, glimmering on the tall chimney-pots, rousing the dozy sparrows to a shrill twittering; and they were hungry and thirsty and dreadfully weary, when they turned another corner and there before them was a huge dining-room table piled with things to eat and drink, and behind it was standing Evangeline. 'Oh, Evangeline,' they cried, 'do give us some!'

But Evangeline only broke into jeering laughter and started capering up and down like a gorilla. She was not looking her loveliest, for her podgy round face was coated with porridge and she wore Mademoiselle's red bonnet, its streamers hanging down in front, like an overgrown balcony. But they were not at their best themselves, with their little golden beards, all wearing Evangeline's horrid red and purple dresses and black button-boots. And when, marking time with running steps just to stay where they were, they grabbed at the food, they found that the sausage-rolls were bandages, really, wound up round nothing; and out of each mug of milk hopped a toad, fat and mottled, and hopped on to their heads and sat croaking dismally among the feathers and flowers of Aunt Adelaide's hats. It was joined there by Parrot and Canary – one Parrot and one Canary for each child; and now they must stagger on to a full orchestration of croaks and chirrups and hoarse cries of 'Anchors aweigh!' And so daylight came.

Daylight came, and they were getting to the outskirts of London, running by strange, twisting routes past the Tower – where the ravens formed an escort for them, dismally croaking; past Hampton Court, where they got into the Maze and ran round and round until they were dizzy. Fortunately, the ravens and Parrot and Canary and the toads got dizzy too, and flapped and hopped away; and when they passed Kew Gardens Great-Aunt Adelaide's flowered hats flew off too, to join their relations in the hothouses. If only they could get to the country and find a herd of goats, perhaps they might even get rid of the little beards!

On and on, through the early-morning suburbs, where the housemaids came out on to the steps in their big aprons and starched white caps, to have their jugs filled by the milkman at the door . . . 'Oh, Mr Milkman, please give us some!' cried the children; but when, smiling, he began to pour out the sweet, fresh-smelling milk – alas! there came a hole in the jug and it all ran through. And he looked down into the jug and cried out: 'They've stolen all the milk. Stop thief!'

Stop thief! The children's hearts rose. 'Yes, yes,' they cried, 'stop us, please stop us, don't let us go on running away!' Even the hulks would be better, even deportation would be better than having to run one single solitary step more. 'Stop us, we're thieves, we've stolen Great-Aunt Adelaide's ear trumpet, don't let us get away!'

Along the clean morning pavements, the fine ladies walked with their gentlemen friends, swan-like in their swirly dresses and high, proud hats. 'Stop them!' they cried to the gentlemen, when

they saw the running children. But the gentlemen turned into big umbrellas and ran after the children and whacked them on the backs of their legs with their own much littler umbrellas. 'Faster, faster!' they cried. 'The sun is high in the sky and the road is getting hotter and hotter; if you don't pick up your feet faster, they'll get burnt. It's as hot as a griddle.' 'You know what we can do about *that*,' said the children, beginning to dance. But now they found themselves caught up by the elbows and scurried this way and that by eager hands; like lumps of something horrible, being pushed about by ants. And voices were crying,

'*C'est par ici! Non, non, c'est par là!*' and they saw that the ladies had turned into dozens and dozens of Mademoiselles all chivvying them down the road to the public loo. 'Well, at least when we get there,' thought the children, 'we'll *have* to stop!'

But someone had exchanged the notices, and out of the one marked GENTLEMEN came Miss Prawn, covered in a lather of cheese, and from the one marked LADIES appeared Professor Schnorr, clad only in his trousers, with his big black beard spread out over his front. But what looked like his tummy was a large, pink sofa cushion, really, and when he saw Miss Prawn, her pale shrimp-pink form glimmering through the decent lather, he flung it from him and bolted off round the corner. The cushion burst and all the feathers flew up in a cloud and settled softly upon lathered Miss Prawn. Like a huge baby gosling covered in down, she flew up urgently cackling into the air; landed again, took one look at the children's legs and with outstretched beak, gave chase.

On and on and on. The last of the houses came and they were out in the country, pounding along the empty lanes between the tall hedges, where the milkwort and ragged robin made all the air sweet with the scent of green juices. They saw Cook and Gumble and Fiddle, carrying trays, but the moment they set eyes on the children they took to their heels and with great kangaroo-hops leapt and lolloped away; and they had been running since bed-time last night – and now it was afternoon.

And suddenly – bowling ahead of them in an open carriage – Mr and Mrs Haversack, with Adolphus sitting squashed in between them. 'Oh, Adolphus, oh, Mr Haversack, oh, Mrs Haversack!' cried the children, catching up with them, jog-trotting along beside the carriage, 'do let us get in with you, do give us a lift, we're so hot and tired and we can't stop running away . . .'

Mrs Haversack bowed to right and left. 'Poor things! What can we do for them, Haversack? Advise me!'

But Mr Haversack only fluffed up his long golden beard and said 'Prrrrrr-up!' and all of a sudden Adolphus was growing strangely black and shiny in the face and his nose was growing longer and stiff whiskers were growing out on either side of it. 'A dolphin! He's turned into a

dolphin!' cried Mrs Haversack, and prodded the coachman in the back with her parasol. 'Quick – to the Zoo!' The children heard his honk-honk-honking as the carriage bowled away.

The long day passed – the long, long, weary day. Evening came. They breasted a hill and came upon a herd of goats, sitting by the roadside, scratching at their flanks with their little black hooves. 'Where are you going?' bleated the goats. 'And why have you got our beards?' 'Line up across the road,' cried the children, 'and stop us running away, and we'll give them back to you.' For they saw now that the goats had indeed no hair upon their chinny-chin-chins.

So the goats lined up across the road and the children stopped (jerking down up and down, marking time, but at least not actually running) and tugged at the beards. And the goats stopped scratching and poked forward their naked chins. And in a little while . . .

In a little while all the goats were bearded, but not scratching any longer with their little polished hooves; and the children had no beards, but scratched as they ran.

Darkness fell and the stars came out and twinkled down upon them; and they ran and they ran and they ran. And someone had cut the elastic of their knickers and the starched, frilly legs had fallen down round their ankles and impeded their every step. 'We know now,' they said, sobbing, to one another, 'how the Baby feels with its nappies always coming down.' And they passed it back, down the long crocodile of stumbling children, the mumbling, grumbling, tumbling children, staggering on, falling, scrambling up again, tripping and regaining their feet once more – 'Poor Baby, now we know how you feel . . .!'

And an idea began to grow. It grew and it grew; starting with the Big Ones, making its way back to the Middling Ones, through the Little Ones, back to the Littlest Ones, right down to the Baby itself, forging along, its fat little elbows going like pistons, on its two little fat, bent legs ... And when the idea came to the Baby it stopped running, absolutely stopped running, in that one moment; and sat down in a round, mournful bundle in the middle of the road and put its round pudding fists in its eyes and sobbed out: 'Wonk Nurk Magiggy! Wairg my Nurk Magiggy?'

And a voice said out of the darkness, and as

velvet as the darkness: 'Darling Baby – I am here.'

And there she was – a warmth, a glow, a golden radiance in the chill and darkness of the night: Nurse Matilda.

And she gave one thump with her stick: and all the children stopped running, and cried out: 'Oh, Nurse Matilda – why didn't we think of you before? Please take us home.'

And Nurse Matilda stood there and smiled at them; and she said, 'Oh, my wicked ones, my naughty, naughty children! – just give me one good reason why I should!'

The children didn't stop to think. They said: 'We were only running away because we didn't want to stay without *you*.'

And Nurse Matilda smiled and smiled; and when she smiled, it seemed to the children that really she must be the loveliest person in all the world. Except . . . Well, really you had to say it: Except for that terrible Tooth.

And at that moment while they were thinking it – couldn't help thinking it – what do you think happened? That Tooth of hers flew out and landed in the middle of the road at the children's feet.

And it began to grow.

It grew and it grew. It grew until it was the size of a matchbox. It grew until it was the size of a snuff-box. It grew until it was the size of a shoe-box − of a tuck-box − of a suitcase − of a packing-case − of a trunk: of a big trunk, a huge trunk, a simply enormous trunk. And all the while as it grew, it was taking shape − growing golden and shining and beautifully curved, growing windows on either side of it, in curly golden frames; growing hollow inside with a soft leather lining: growing big golden wheels: growing a coachman sitting up on the box above it, growing a footman in frogged coat and plush breeches, standing holding the door: growing a team of six beautiful horses, tossing their proud heads, stamping their shining hooves, jingling their harness, eager to be off. And into the coach climbed Nurse Matilda, carrying the sleepy Baby in her arms; and after her climbed the children, one after the other, pushing in, piling in and yet seeming each to find a comfortable place with lots of room; all clustered round Nurse Matilda as she sat in the centre of the soft, leather-backed seat; curled up around her, sleepily, safely, like

drowsy bees round a golden honey-pot. And clip clop, clip clop, went the shining hooves, and nid-nod, nid-nod, went the droopy heads . . . And there came a big gate – but it wasn't Great-Aunt Adelaide's gate; and there was a curving drive up to a big front door, standing wide open; and shining down at them were the friendly, welcoming, lighted windows – of their own dear home!

And – how could it have happened that, to each child, it seemed as if loving arms came around him and he was lifted up gently and his weary head cradled against a kind shoulder? And

he was carried softly and silently into the house
and up the wide stairs and slipped into his own
warm cosy bed: washed and brushed and changed
into night clothes, teeth cleaned, prayers said and
peacefully dreaming . . . Dreaming that he was
running away: but would wake up in his own bed
in the morning, all safe and sound – only quite,
quite certain never to run away again.

When they did wake up next morning – Nurse
Matilda was gone.

NURSE MATILDA
GOES TO HOSPITAL

To darling Lucy
and to Danny and Joel
and to all the other children
who know that I am a whych

Chapter 1

NCE upon a time there were a mother and father called Mr and Mrs Brown and they had lots and lots of children; and all the children were terribly, terribly naughty.

One wintry Sunday, Mrs Brown went up to the schoolroom to speak to her children and this is what they were doing:

Tora had fastened a melting icicle to the back of Nanny's skirt and everywhere Nanny went she found, to her great alarm, that she was leaving a little wet dribble.

Jake had nailed a bit of fish to the underneath side of the big round schoolroom table and no one could think where the awful smell was coming from.

Joel had put glue in the girls' woolly outdoor gloves and now, however much Nanny crossly told them to take them off, the poor things couldn't.

*All the other children were doing simply dreadful
things too.*

Mrs Brown was very sweet but she really was
rather foolish about her dear, darling children, and
never could believe that they could be really
naughty. So she said: 'Good morning, Nanny, I
hope the children are behaving themselves?'

'Yes, Madam,' said Nanny gloomily, hoping Mrs
Brown wouldn't notice the little dribble or the
strong smell of fish or the fact that all her
daughters appeared to have developed large, hairy,
coloured hands.

'Well, then, children, I have a lovely surprise for
you,' said Mrs Brown. 'What do you think? Nurse
Matilda is coming to tea.'

Some of *you* children will have read about how
Nurse Matilda came to the naughty Brown
children and made them all good again. She was
dreadfully ugly but as they got gooder and
gooder, she got prettier and prettier until at last
she was really lovely and all surrounded by a sort
of golden glow. But I'm afraid that when she
went away, the children always got naughty all
over again.

However, they were delighted that she was

coming to see them. 'We had better not go to Sunday School,' they said, piously, 'but stay at home and put on our best clothes for Nurse Matilda.'

'Beck cloag for Nurk Magiggy,' echoed the Baby. It was a splendid baby and talked a language all of its own. It wore an untidy bundle of nappies which always looked as though they were going to come down, but never quite did.

'That will be lovely,' said Mrs Brown, very proud that they should have thought of putting on their best clothes, which they loathed – and quite right too, because they were simply hideous. 'But I think you'll be able to fit in Sunday School too.'

'Oh, *lor*'!' said the children, not piously at all.

So after midday dinner, they formed into a long crocodile and went off through the snow to the church hall, driven from behind by Nanny; (her boots had by now filled with water from the melted icicle and she was very uncomfortable and couldn't make it out at *all*). The village children stood by to cheer them on their resentful way, led by their greatest enemy, a large and horrible boy called Podge Green; all leaping up and down sticking out their tongues and calling out, 'Yah-yah – goody-goodies!' 'You just wait!' muttered the crocodile, filing by, showing all its teeth.

The Vicar, whose name was Mr Privy, had planned a little lecture about Loving Thy Neighbour, and had even made up a special hymn, beginning, '*Children who are kind and meek, And always turn the other cheek, Will fill their lives with merry fun, And be belov'd by everyone.*' He sometimes felt that it was not very likely that the Brown children would ever be belov'd by everyone, or even anyone at all, especially by himself. However, he had even made up a tune to go with his hymn and all the mothers and children in the class stood up to sing it.

The Brown children, however, who perhaps were not quite so kind and meek as they should have been, always sang whatever hymn they chose and that was what finally won; for they simply sang away, never mind what music was being played or what the other people were singing, and there were so many of them that in the end everyone else gave up and joined in with *them*. So they now sang Onward Christian Soldiers at the tops of their voices, and this, I must say, did make it rather a bad start for Mr Privy and his little talk about living at peace with one's neighbour; especially, he thought to himself, if one's neighbour was the Browns.

He embarked upon it at last, however, with a look towards them that suggested that he might profit by the lesson himself. The children gazed back at him with innocent faces, meanwhile keeping up a muffled underground hullabaloo, the boys playing a kind of soccer with their caps between the rows of chairs, the girls poking under the seats with their umbrellas at the legs of the people in front of them. . . . 'Emma! Susie! Tim! Be-*have*!' hissed Nanny, squelching angrily up and down the aisle with her boots full of water.

Clemency stood up in her place. She said to Mr Privy in a very loud, clear voice, 'I can't hear what you're saying?'

Charlotte shot up in *her* place. 'Neither can I.'

'Neither can we,' cried all the Brown children.

'Oh, dear, that will never do! I'll try to speak louder,' said Mr Privy. He proceeded on his discourse in a rousing bellow. 'We still can't hear,' complained the children, bellowing back.

Poor Mr Privy threw a great deal of expression into his words, twisting his poor face into knots in his effort to make himself understood. 'He looks like a mad horse,' whispered Jennifer. All along the rows of seats, the children burst into muffled giggles, passing the message along. 'Ara*bella*! Cla*rissa*! Se*bas*tian!' hissed Nanny, dashing squelch, squelch from one side of the aisle to the other, 'I said *bee-have*!'

'Why does she keep saying bee-hive?' said Roger. Goodness, he added thoughtfully, suppose there was a swarm of bees!

'A swarm! Ow-ow!' cried all the children immediately. 'A swarm of bees! Nanny says there's

a swarm of bees!' and they flapped their hands in front of their faces to drive away the imaginary bees.

'Bees?' cried the lady in the front bench, turning round with an anxious look.

'Yes, bees. And, excuse me,' said Christianna, politely, 'but you've got one too. You've got a bee in your bonnet,' and she leaned forward and kindly tried to brush the bee off. But she only succeeded in brushing off the bonnet and several bits of the lady's hair with it. 'Look out, look out!' cried the Little Ones helpfully, in high shrill voices. 'A bee will sting your bald head!' The lady clapped back the bonnet, bits of hair and all and, holding it on with one hand, flapped wildly round the heads of her own children. 'Lucy, Thomas, Victoria, William! Be careful, you'll get stung. . .!' The children next to Lucy and Thomas and Victoria and William began to flap too, passing on the alarming news . . . The Brown children set up a steady, humming bzz-bzzzz.

Up on the platform, Mr Privy, deafened to all this sound and confusion by his own attempt to shout loud enough, stopped at last and peered down over the tops of his glasses. His whole

Sunday school seemed suddenly to have gone mad: rising up in their seats and dancing about in the most extraordinary fashion, waving their arms above their heads with looks of extreme terror on their poor pale faces. Several of those dreadful – those *dear, sweet* Brown children, said Mr Privy to himself, remembering just in time his own talk about loving your neighbour – had got hold of the little black velvet butterfly nets on the ends of long sticks which were used in the church next door to collect the Sunday offerings – and were chasing up and down swatting at the air with increasingly unbridled cries of, 'Missed it!' and 'Got it!' – and rushing to the windows and shaking something out of the bags and dashing back for more. 'Got *what?*' cried poor Mr Privy, peering this way and that. 'Bees!' cried the audience back to him. 'A plague of bees! The whole place is swarming with them, take care, you'll get stung!' And they began to leap up and down more agitatedly than ever at the idea of their own dear Vicar a prey to bees, and to cry out to the children with the butterfly nets to rescue him.

'Rescue the Vicar! Rescue Mr Privy!' cried the

Brown children, delighted at the idea. With Pam and Simon in the lead, half a dozen of them crept up on to the platform. Simon took a great swipe.

The velvet bag was not very strongly sewn on, for it came away quite easily from its ring and remained sitting on top of Mr Privy's head like a little black nightcap. The ring, still on its long handle, went on down round his neck. He said in a voice by no means filled with love for Simon: 'GET – IT – OFF!'

The children hung on to their end of the handle and tried to get the ring off: but the ring wouldn't come. They pulled it this way, and nearly flattened Mr Privy's nose against his face, they pushed it that way and half lifted him off his feet by the ears – but it wouldn't come. Caro said at last: 'We shall have to get some soap.'

'Soap?' choked the Vicar. The metal ring had got lodged between his teeth now, like a horse's bit.

'To make your face more slide-y,' explained Lindy kindly.

So Christianna produced some soap from the vestry next door and they soon had a fine lather all over Mr Privy's face; snowflakes of it drifted about the room as he puffed and blew, struggling like anything to get away from their kind ministrations. They had to give up in the end and, leading him like an angry little bull at the end of a rigid halter, got him down from the platform and disappeared with him into the vestry. Muffled cries of 'Ow! Ow!' echoed through the hall – at first from Mr Privy and then, I am sorry to say, from the children. I don't think Mr Privy had profited one bit from his own lesson about loving everybody. After all, they were only trying to rescue him from the bees.

Meanwhile, Podge Green and his friends had been waiting at the lych gate of the church, rather anxious and beginning to wish they had not pulled the crocodile's tail quite so hard. 'We must arm ourselves with lots of snowballs,' said Podge, assuming the leadership in a very important manner.

It seemed a long time before the children came out of the church hall, and in fact it was. The Vicar, muttering urgently to himself that he must try to love his neighbour even if it was one of the Browns, was standing in the door-way shaking hands with all the mothers and children as they passed out, and speaking a kindly word. The Brown children, eager to see how long he could keep this up, were filing by and immediately running round and re-joining the end of the queue. By the time he had shaken hands four times each with every one of them, and spoken a fourth kind word, he was – though much delighted at such a large attendance to his Sunday School – getting tired and rather cross. And so was Nanny, who had to keep running round after her charges and getting her hand shaken and a kindly word, time after time; when all she wanted to do was to chivvy them all home and change into dry boots.

Podge Green and his army stood beside their fine big heaps of snowballs. 'Here they come!'

This time Nanny was in the lead with the Little Ones trotting behind her, holding hands in angelic pairs. The first snowball took her bonk! on the nose and was followed by such a hail of snow that when she looked back, the babies had entirely disappeared and there was only a long, white, writhing monster uttering muffled cries of 'Let us out!' So much occupied was she in dashing up and

273

down brushing the snow off the tops of their heads, that she did not see that Podge's army was in full flight down the hill pursued by the Middling Ones and the Big Ones of the Brown family.

Podge Green's mother and father ran the sweet shop in the village and Podge and his friends ate far too much biscuit and chocolate and were all very fat; though none was nearly as fat as Podge himself. Being so stout, they couldn't run very fast and soon fell over their own feet and went rolling off down the hill, gathering snow as they went, until they were nothing but huge, round snowballs themselves – spinning at a great rate and ending up with a bonk against the wall at the bottom. But Podge was *so* fat that his head and feet were right up off the ground and he finished up like a sort of rolling-pin, with his head and feet like the rolling-pin handles, sticking out at both ends. Upon these ends the Brown children seized joyfully and, leaving the others lolling like broken snowmen against the wall, they trundled him through the village towards their own gate.

The snow had melted here and little bits of gravel from the road stuck to Podge as he rolled. By the time they came to the top of their drive, he looked as if he had been egg-and-breadcrumbed, all ready to be fried. He could have done with some frying, as a matter of fact. 'Ow, ow!' he cried. 'I'm *cold*!'

'I expect your blood is frozen in your veins,' said the children standing round him cheerfully. 'We shall have to make a hole in you and light a little fire and boil it up a bit,' and they trundled the rolling-pin round to the back door and began to haul and push it, melting rapidly, up the back stairs. Hoppit the butler and Cook, and Hortense the lady's maid, and Alice-and-Emily the parlour maids, would be safely out of the way having a Sunday afternoon snooze; ('Drat that Nanny!' said Cook later to Hoppit, 'she must have dribbled the whole way up them back stairs. They're all wet. Whatever can be the matter with her?')

The children got Podge into the schoolroom and heaved him up, stiff as a board, on to the table. 'We shall need some very large kitchen knives to cut him open with,' said Stephanie. 'And some boiling water to unfreeze his inside with,' said Sarah. 'And some needles and cotton to sew him up again,' said Sophie. 'Or what about some glue?' said Hetty. 'Ow, ow, *ow*!' said Podge.

So Fenella went down to the kitchen and returned with some of Cook's aprons and Dominic made some of Hortense's stiff, starchy white caps into splendid surgeons' masks, and Christopher, who was not exactly a good speller, went outside and with a piece of chalk drew a large red cross on the schoolroom door and wrote in big letters: HOSPIDILT. '*Now!*' they said to Podge.

And at that moment from outside came Mrs Brown's voice, saying, 'Children? Have you forgotten you're expecting a visitor?' And the door flew open. And there she stood, smiling and lovely and all in her golden glow. Nurse Matilda!

'Nurk Magiggy!' cried the Baby joyfully. 'Ick my Nurk Magiggy!' 'Oh, yes,' cried all the children. 'It's Nurse Matilda!'

Nurse Matilda took one look around her – at the girls in their nurses' aprons, at the boys in their surgeons' masks – at Podge lying trussed up in a pool of melting snow and little stones; at the notice on the door. And the glow went out; and suddenly Nurse Matilda wasn't pretty any more – but a small, stout, ugly person carrying a big black stick – what Nurse Matilda could do with that

big black stick! She wore a rusty black dress that came up to her neck and right down to her black button boots, and a rusty black bonnet all trembly with jet, with the bun of her hair sticking out at the back like a teapot handle. And her face was very brown and wrinkly and her eyes were very small and black and shiny; and her nose! — her nose was like two potatoes. But what you noticed most of all about her was her Tooth — one huge front tooth, sticking right out like a tombstone over her lower lip. . . .

'*Well!*' said Nurse Matilda. And she lifted up her big black stick and gave one thump on the schoolroom floor.

Chapter 2

BANG! went the big black stick; and all of a sudden there came a clanging of bells and rattling of wheels over the frozen roads, and a scuttering of gravel as horses' hooves pulled up on the drive beneath the schoolroom window; and great cries of 'Get out the stretchers! Where's the medicine! Have some bowls ready in case they're sick!' And the children looked at each other and looked down their own fronts – and saw that everyone was in a dressing-gown and bedroom slippers, with a neat little parcel of washing things in one hand.

And they looked out of the window and there, lined up before the front door, was a whole fleet of horse-drawn ambulances. And they knew that the worst had happened. They had teased poor fat Podge about being in hospital and now Nurse

Matilda had banged with her big black stick – and here they were in dressing-gowns all ready to go into hospital themselves!

'Or going inkoo hokkigig?' said the Baby, raising its wondering big blue eyes to Nurse Matilda. 'In our jenking-gowns?'

Nurse Matilda looked down at it and just for a moment she smiled a tiny little smile; and she lifted up the Baby in her arms and stood with it held close and safe against her rusty black shoulder – and moved back and out of the way. And in through the door poured a horde of white-coated men who snatched the children up in pairs and laid them on to stretchers and scurried off down the stairs and hoisted them into ambulances and dashed back again for more. 'Hey, what are you doing? – there's nothing wrong with *us*!' cried the children, anxiously. 'Tonsils this lot!' cried the stretcher-bearers over their heads, taking no notice; or, 'Appendicitis, these three!' or, 'Medical wards, those ones there, they only need lots of Doses . . .!' 'No we don't,' cried the children, 'we're perfectly well, we don't need operations and we certainly don't need Doses!' They had in the past had experience of Nurse Matilda's medicine.

But nobody took any notice. Soon the attendants climbed in, one to each ambulance, and the doors were slammed shut and off they went, the horses clattering gaily down the drive and out through the village, with the children bumping resentfully behind. 'Well, there's one thing,' they said to each other, 'when we get to the hospital, Nurse Matilda won't be there with her big black stick. You don't have children's nurses in hospitals.' And they began to think of naughty things to do when they got there.

In fact, they could think of some naughty things to do right now . . . 'Ow! Ow!' cried all the children in the leading ambulance. 'Stop the ambulance, quick!'

'What for?' cried the ambulance men, alarmed.

'Ow! Ow!' cried the children, not answering directly. 'Stop the ambulance, stop the ambulance!'

So the ambulance stopped and the ambulances behind it had to stop too; and in a minute the children had all jumped out and were seizing the ambulance men and tying them up with bandages and lying them down on the bunks, well wrapped up in red hospital blankets; and

Anthony and Edward and Justin had jumped up on the driving seats and were saying 'Chk, Chk!' to the horses and hoping they would just trot on ahead which, being nice horses, was what they did.

The hospital was a very big white building full of tidy white beds, hungry for patients. But the people who lived all round seemed to be dreadfully healthy and lots of the beds were empty. The surgeons and doctors and nurses were simply longing for more people to chop up and dose and tuck into the tidy white beds; and quite a cheer arose from the Staff, assembled on the wide front steps as the first of the ambulances appeared.

Eager hands pulled open the doors and lifted out the stretchers. 'M'f,m'f,m'f,' cried the occupant of the first stretcher in an angry voice muffled by tightly tucked-in red blankets. 'Don't you worry, everything will be quite all right,' said the hospital porters, humping the stretcher cheerfully up the steps. 'M'f,m'f,*m'f*!' insisted the patient desperately. 'Oh, they all say that, but you'll simply love it really,' cried all the nurses and surgeons and doctors; and, terrified that one of their victims would rebel and jump up off the stretcher and get away, they all helped to bundle it on to a sort of thing on wheels and bowl it away down the corridor. 'Immediate operation!' panted the ambulance attendant, lolloping along, keeping pace with it, though he kept falling over his white coat which seemed to be much too long.

'No time to waste!' 'Emergency!' cried all the surgeons joyfully and began to race one another down the long corridors, pulling on their brown rubber gloves as they went. '*M'f,m'f,M'F!*' yelled the poor patient through mouthfuls of red blanket.

The surgeon who got there first was the top one of the lot; his name was Sir Minsupp Izgizzard. He took no notice at all of m'f,m'f, m'fs, but seized up a huge knife and was just about to chop up the patient right, left and centre when he suddenly remembered that he didn't know what was wrong with him. 'What's wrong with you?' he said.

'*M'f*-m'f,' said the patient.

'It can't be nothing or you wouldn't be here. Now take that thing out of your mouth,' said Sir Minsupp impatiently, 'and tell me plainly what's the matter.' But he now observed that the patient's arms were tightly strapped down to his sides and he hastily unbuckled them. 'Good heavens!' he said. '*You're* not a patient. You're the ambulance attendant. Why didn't you say so?' And he dropped everything and rushed back to the front door steps. 'Look out!' he cried. 'They're up to mischief! Don't let any of them get away . . .!'

All the surgeons and the doctors and the nurses turned round to hear what he was saying. By the time they turned back again, another patient had been carried up on a stretcher; and a rather small coachman in a very large coachman's hat and coat was driving away the second ambulance. 'M'f, m'f, m'f!' cried the patient. 'I've heard that before! Follow that ambulance!' cried Sir Minsupp. Out of the ambulance windows peered the faces of a dozen children all crammed in for the get-away. 'Oh well,' they said to each other, as the surgeons and nurses and doctors caught up with them, 'we'll have to think of something naughty to do once we're *in*.' They thought they might just manage to think of something.

I think the last ambulance-full of children were really the best – or the worst, I suppose I ought to say. When Sir Minsupp Izgizzard finally got the patient on to the operating table – after the most fearful struggle going on under the red blankets and M'f,m'f,m'fs in the most *extraordinary* voice – he discovered (only just in time) that he was taking out the tonsils of one of the ambulance horses! (The horse simply loved it and ever afterwards bored all the other horses by insisting upon telling about 'my operation'.)

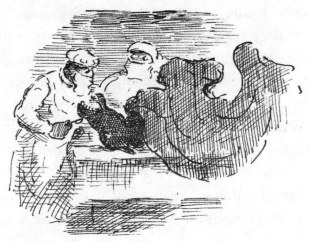

By supper time, the hospital had more or less settled down again. The ambulance men had been sorted out and were conducting a meeting about how they could all get different jobs, the horse was back in the stables making dreadful puns about, 'I kept telling them I was only a little hoarse, but they still took out my tonsils. . . .' and the Brown children were tucked up among various other patients in several wards.

All the wards – fortunately for the children – radiated off a sort of central hall, like the spokes of a wheel; so they weren't too far from each other. Podge Green had been gathered up with the rest of them and was in a corner bed stodging down the hospital supper which was simply horrible fish and rice pudding – to Podge any food was better than no food; and the Baby had a little cot where it spent its time standing up watching everything over the top rail, with its nappies coming down round its fat, bent knees as usual.

When Staff Nurse arrived to announce Matron's Round, this is what the children were doing:

Joanna had scraped up the uneaten rice pudding from all the plates and stuffed it into a spare pillow case.

Louisa and Rebecca had collected the bunches of grapes which the patients' kind relatives had brought them, and were treading them into wine in a hospital hip-bath.

Daniel had swapped round all the charts at the heads of the patients' beds which told what was wrong with them, and added a few suggestions of his own.

Romilly had turned the Little Ones' cots upside down and made sort of wooden cages out of them; and the Little Ones were pretending to be in a zoo.

All the other children were doing simply dreadful things too.

Staff Nurse was very round and red and when she was cross she could give a very loud bellow. She gave a very loud one indeed when she saw Rebecca and Louisa treading wine in the middle of her ward. They skipped pretty quickly back into bed, with their feet bright purple from the grapes. 'All sit up straight and tidy,' said Staff Nurse. 'Matron will be making her Rounds.' She caught up the temperature chart of one of the elderly patients. 'A hundred and four! What are you sitting up for? You'll kill yourself.'

'You told me to,' said the patient. 'You've just said to sit up straight.'

'Well then, lie down straight,' said Staff Nurse, crossly. She whipped up another chart. 'My goodness, Mrs Bloggs, you *are* getting better! You can jump up and help to clear away the supper trays.'

Of course poor Mrs Bloggs's chart had been mixed up by Daniel with somebody else's. 'I can't,' she said, reeling round and round in little circles, quite dizzy with temperature. 'My head's buzzing like a bee-hive.'

'Nonsense,' said Staff Nurse. 'You mustn't imagine things. It says here on your chart that you're perfectly normal.' She marched off into one of the boy's wards. 'Eaten up all your nice supper? Good! All nice and comfortable?'

'Ibe dot,' said Podge. He was still very chilly from being made a rolling-pin out of, and had already developed a cold in his nose. 'I'be very *ud*cubfortable.'

'Nonsense!' said Staff Nurse again. Nobody was allowed to be uncomfortable in *her* ward. 'Here – have another pillow!' She picked up one that seemed to be spare and put it behind his head with an angry pat. 'Matron will be round in a minute and I want you all to be enjoying yourselves. *En-joy*ing yourselves,' she repeated glaring round at them, daring them to feel ill or miserable.

'Yes, Nurse,' said the patients obediently, though they felt that they might be going to enjoy themselves even less now that the Brown children had arrived. 'You will love Matron,' they added to the children, hoping to impress them all into good behaviour. 'So kind –'

'So gentle –'

'Florence Nightingale herself –'

And here was Matron, bearing down upon them along the corridor like a liner coming into port with sisters and nurses and junior doctors like little tugs, fussing around her; hooting Yes Matron, No Matron, as they advanced. 'Well, Staff Nurse – everything going smoothly?'

'Yes Matron, No Matron,' said Staff Nurse, catching the infection. They all came to a halt in the little central hall and Matron turned slowly round and looked down the long length of each of the wards. 'Um – not exactly *smoothly*, Matron,' said Staff Nurse, making up her mind.

'H'm,' said Matron spinning slowly to look into the first ward.

Mrs Bloggs was still spinning. She had got out of bed, as instructed by Staff Nurse, and was now going round and round in little circles, carrying a supper tray and buzzing away happily to herself, her face quite crimson with high temperature but very glad to have been told by Staff Nurse that she was perfectly well. Further down the ward, however, an anxious lady called Miss Fizzle was lying back against her pillows in a terrible taking because *her* temperature had apparently shot up to a hundred and four. She had struggled up and read the chart at the head of her bed and besides having all Mrs Bloggs's troubles listed on it, the children had added a few suggestions of their own. Over opposite, a stout old lady also was struggling out of bed, crying, 'Let me go, let me go before it's too late . . .!' Goodness knows what the children had written on *her* chart!

In the middle of the ward was a hip-bath full of squashed grapes; and Louisa and Sarah were pretending to be fast asleep with purple feet sticking out from under their blankets . . .

Matron took one long look – at Mrs Bloggs, spinning, at Miss Fizzle studying her chart with a face as flat and white as a pancake, at the stout old lady heaving herself out of bed and streaking down the ward in her red flannel nightie, crying, 'Let me out, let me out!' – at the two pairs of purple feet and the hip-bath . . .

And she turned and looked into the second ward.

Chapter 3

WHILE Staff Nurse was busy in the Women's Ward, this is what the children had been doing in the Men's.

Daniel had altered the patients' charts in there too.

Matthew had changed round the little bed-side lockers where the patients kept their private possessions.

Flavia had tied the cords of their dressing-gowns to the ends of their beds

And Hannah and Joel had got in under the blankets of one of the spare beds and were heaving up and down giving the effect of a very terrible bright red monster. . . .

All the other children had done dreadful things too.

Matron stood in the doorway.

Things in here were almost worse than in the

Women's Ward. Several old gentlemen were in full flight, trying to get out of hospital because of the awful things Danny had written on their charts. But as they struggled into their dressing-gowns, they found them suddenly much too large or much too small, and they were in a terrible taking because they thought they had contracted some dread disease which made them shrink – or swell up – all in a minute. And they foraged in their lockers for their slippers and the ones with too-tight dressing-gowns found that their slippers were too big and the ones with their dressing-gowns too big found that their slippers were much too tight; so they thought that all the rest of them had swelled and their feet had shrunk, or the other way about. 'Ow! Ow!' they cried, jostling each other to escape, convinced that they would shrink right down into pygmies (with huge feet) or swell right up into giants (with tiny ones) and be exhibited in circuses for the rest of their lives. 'Let us out! Let us out!' But the cords of their dressing-gowns were tied to their beds and now they either found themselves yanked back and in bed again or – if they were (really) rather fat and strong – towing their beds behind them. 'Ow, ow, *ow*!' cried these ones, even louder, at finding that their beds seemed to be following them about where ever they went, longing to gobble them back in again; and 'Ow, *ow*, OW!' they cried when they saw the Monster bed, with Hannah and Daniel threshing about underneath the red blankets, uttering the huge, hungry growls of a dragon intent upon its prey. Vicky and Tim were kindly dashing about amongst the rest of the patients with basins in case they wanted to be sick. The patients hadn't had the smallest desire to be sick but the sight of the basins made them feel horribly queasy and they joined in the general moaning and groaning and cries of ow, ow, ow!

In the third ward, the upside-down cots had settled into quite a realistic zoo and the Littlest Ones were rampaging up and down behind the

bars, growling and roaring in a very terrible manner and demanding their dinners with a tremendous gnashing of teeth. This greatly alarmed the grown-up patients, who kept poking up scared white faces to see what was happening. Toni, David and Jaci were keeping the animals at bay, banging about with some spare crutches they had found lying around (to the great rage of the one-legged patients, who urgently needed them) and crying: 'Hup! Hup!' and 'Watch that leopard!' and 'They're trying to get at the patients!' and other encouraging remarks. 'The wild beasts have got the children!' cried the patients, seeing the wheels of the cots spinning idly in the air. 'Naughty tiger, let go of that little boy's leg!' cried Toni and Jaci and David immediately, upon hearing this, and 'Now, Leo, one arm will be quite enough for you . . .!' 'After all, they have to be fed,' they said kindly to the patients. 'Oh, dear, when they've finished, they'll start upon us,' cried the one-legged patients, hopping about this way and that, banging into one another and hopping off again. In his corner, stout Podge hid his head under his rice-pudding pillow, bringing it out now and again to take a deep breath and plunge it back once more. He knew that out of all the patients, any lion or tiger in its senses must choose *him* as the fattest and tastiest.

Matron stood in the little central hall. A cot shot past her nose, containing the Baby, swinging happily like a monkey against its bars, crooning a little song, being whizzed back and forth most soothingly along the polished floors, down one ward – a good push from any child that happened to be there – across the hall, down the other ward – a good push from any child that happened to be *there* – and back again.

'Well!' said Matron; and she began to look not at all gentle and saintly and just like Florence Nightingale; but very black and cross indeed. She said to Staff Nurse: 'What is *this*?'

A long train of beds shot past, narrowly missing the Baby in its zooming cot. The children had tied them all together with bandages and were giving the unwilling patients lovely rides, with great ringings of the dinner bell and shoutings of: 'Allstationsto—*Woant*hurt, *Ly*still, *Bee*sick and *Bed*pan . . . All change at *Big*dose, *Little*pill and Wantergotethe*loo* . . .' Susannah had tied the nurses' apron strings into one big knot and they were struggling furiously in the middle of the ward like a huge, angry octopus, trying to tear itself apart.

Matron looked into the three wards – at Mrs Bloggs circling and buzzing, at Miss Fizzle fuming, at the poor old lady streaking off in her red flannel nightie: at the hip-bath and the purple feet . . . At the old gentlemen scuttling this way and that in their too-tight slippers and their too-big dressing-gowns, towing heaving beds behind them, or being swallowed back in; at the green faces bending over unwanted basins, at the spinning cot wheels and the cages underneath, with their menagerie of Little Ones squealing and growling and gnashing their teeth for their dinners of patients' legs and arms . . . At Podge's round behind stuck up into the air as he crouched with his ostrich head buried under his pillow: at the Baby's cot whizzing innocently back and fore, back and fore – at the octopus of nurses and the train of beds . . . And to the other patients she may still have looked very saintly and gentle and kind, but suddenly, to the children–

Suddenly to the children, she looked – well, she looked like a small, stout, elderly person with a

rusty black dress under her starched white hospital apron, and a bun like a teapot-handle beneath her white nurse's cap; and a nose like two potatoes; and, sticking out over her under-lip, a single, huge big tooth . . .

Nurse Matilda!

'Oh, *lor*'!' said the children; and Nurse Matilda lifted up her big black stick.

Nurse Matilda lifted up her big black stick – and suddenly everything seemed to have changed. Mrs Bloggs was back in her bed again with her poor red face and her high temperature, but happily tucked up and not buzzing a bit. And Miss Fizzle was back in *her* bed, murmuring, 'Temperature normal, home tomorrow,' and as pleased as punch. And all the red flannel nighties were back in *their* beds, not wanting to run away any more; and so were all the old gentlemen in the ward next door. And the Little Ones' cots were the right way up again, and they were all cozed up, fast asleep. And all the other children – well, all the other children were lying back against cool white pillows and nurses were advancing upon them with nice hot drinks . . . It was rather surprising because usually when Nurse Matilda banged with her big black stick, things were not comfortable at all. But still, there they were.

All except Podge Green. Podge still crouched with his head under his pillow, breathing heavily from the cold in his nose and not knowing that the zoo noises had ceased and all was safe again. 'Come dear,' said Staff Nurse going over to him, 'this isn't the way to lie at all. Be a good boy and turn over.' And she gave his striped, round pyjama-bottom a playful smack.

Podge gave one shriek of terror and heaved up in his bed. 'Ow, ow! The adibals have got be! The liods are upod be! I've beed bitted by a tiger, the hippobotobus has bodked be with ids hard, hard hoof, the rhidoscerous has biffed be with ids hard, hard hord . . .'

'Now, now, nonsense!' said Staff Nurse. 'There are no animals here, there never have been, you are perfectly safe. Come, turn over, there's a dear!' Trying to heave him up was a bit like wrestling with a huge, striped boiled pudding, but she got him into a sitting position at last. 'Now, then, dear – lean back!'

All round the wards, the children peered forward, their fists stuffed into their mouths to stop themselves from laughing. Podge gazed resentfully back at them, gave one big, resentful sniff and, exhausted, flopped back against the pillow . . .

'Don't trouble, Staff Nurse. Even if it takes them all night,' said Matron quietly, from her place in the central hall, 'the children will clear up the mess for you.'

You wouldn't have thought that in all the world – let alone in one pillow-case – there could have been so much cold, cloggy, sticky, clinging-to-things, *horrible* rice pudding.

From that day on, the children were so good in

hospital that the nurses, and even Staff Nurse, began to expect little white feathery wings to grow up out of their shoulders any minute. They learnt how to make hospital beds and helped in taking round the meals and cups of tea; and their cheerful shouts of 'Bedpan for Mrs Inagonies!' and 'Quick, quick, he's going to be sick!' would echo down the wards to the great comfort of those in emergency. True, they made some mistakes. Told to give Mrs Chumping an air-ring to sit on, they thought Sister had said 'an airing' and wheeled her out into the garden and raced her round and round in her invalid chair. And when Nurse patted Mr Stout's fat tummy and said he would have to diet, they thought she meant 'dye it' and stripped the struggling old gentleman down and painted him a lively blue. But they were very sorry when they discovered they'd been wrong, and dashed Mrs Chumping back into the ward at the rate of knots (no need to dye *her* blue: she had gone a deep shade of indigo with cold and terror) and stripped Mr Stout down all over again and scrubbed him back to pink. So all in all, a time came when the hospital wondered how it had ever got on without the dear, useful, kindly Brown children; and Nurse Matilda grew less and less ugly every day until she became quite pretty; and then she got prettier and prettier . . .

And then . . .

And then one day Mr and Mrs Brown arrived to see their dear, darling children and their dear, darling children seemed to have got over all their illnesses and operations but they were also getting over being quite so good and Nurse Matilda, I'm afraid, was beginning to look rather more like her old self: very black and cross with her big tooth sticking out in front and her bun of hair sticking out at the back like a teapot-handle; and her nose like two potatoes. 'I think,' she said to Mr and Mrs Brown, 'that it is time the children Had a Change.'

'They could go and stay with their Great-Aunt Adelaide Stitch,' said Mrs Brown. 'She has taken rooms at a seaside hotel with Evangeline and Miss Prawn. I'm sure they'd love to have the children.' The hospital would be sorry to see them go, she added: I told you that she really was rather foolish about her dear, darling children. But still she wasn't quite as foolish as all *that*. 'Perhaps it would be safest if you were to go with them,' she said to Nurse Matilda.

Most children have one fearsome aunt and the Browns had this truly fearsome great-aunt, Great-Aunt Adelaide Stitch. She was very gaunt and tall, with an angry little eye like the eye of a rhinoceros, and her nose was like a rhinoceros horn, only turned upside-down. She was extremely short sighted, which the children often found convenient; and very hard of hearing – she used a large ear trumpet rather like a one-horned cow. She had long ago adopted a little girl called Evangeline who, from being quite a nice, cheerful little lump, had turned into a very stout little, horrid little prig; but fortunately, just what Great-Aunt Adelaide liked. Evangeline had a poor, sad governess called Miss Prawn who, summer and winter alike, suffered quite dreadfully from chilblains on her hands; and a simply horrible pug, which with great imagination was called Pug. The children did not want to go and stay with Great-Aunt Adelaide and Evangeline and Pug and Miss Prawn one bit; but still, it was the seaside and much better than the time they had had to stay with them in town. In fact now that they thought of it, the seaside might be quite fun; and as a matter of fact, the town holiday had been quite fun too – for the children, if not for Great-Aunt Adelaide and Evangeline and Pug and Miss Prawn.

So they said goodbye to Staff Nurse and all the other nurses and the patients and prepared to go. Matron seemed to have disappeared; but Nurse Matilda was all ready in her black button boots and rusty black jacket and rusty black bonnet all trimmed with trembly black jet. Outside the hospital stood a line of cabs called 'growlers' with rather weary looking horses, waiting to take them to the station.

'We can't all fit into those cabs,' said the children. 'The horses are too tired.'

'Nonsense,' said all the grown-ups. 'Get in at once.'

'Oh, dear!' said the children, patting the horses' necks and kissing their soft, pink, velvety noses with their tickle-y whiskers. 'We're sorry. But what can we do?'

'Whrrrrrrr!' said the horses, blowing back softly into their faces.

'Good idea!' said the children; and when the time came, piled obediently into the cabs.

But the good idea had been to take the floorboards out of the cabs; so all the children's feet went right through and they ran along gaily (only squashed into rather tight bundles) behind the horses and really were no weight at all. The baby, whose fat little feet wouldn't reach the ground, got carried along, held up by the crush of children in the cab; its short legs whizzing round and round like the wheels of a clockwork engine picked up off the rails.

How Nurse Matilda managed, I'm not quite sure.

Chapter 4

HE station was very exciting, so huge and dim and noisy, with great clouds of steam blowing from the funnels of the engines and a lovely country smell of stables – all the heavy bales and parcels for the goods trains were brought by horse and cart and their stables were lined along the edge of the station. Almond and Agatha almost got left behind, they were so happy talking to the horses; but Nurse Matilda gathered them all together in the end and they filed into the carriages, packed tight together and swinging their feet, delighted to be going off to the seaside at last. The train seemed a bit less delighted; it gave a frightful shriek, as though at the idea of quite so many passengers at one time, and blew off a great deal of steam and a shower of sparks; but the guard wouldn't have any nonsense and waved his green flag in a commanding manner and it began to back out of the station and at last to gather speed, clackety-clack, clackety-clack, clackety-clack – rushing through the country side – dashing into tunnels, screaming at the dark – coming out again into the day-light, on and on and on. Showers of smut and sparks flew out of its funnels and soon the children's faces were covered with little specks like black measles, which made agreeable smudges if you rubbed them with your fingers, especially on each others' faces. By the time they emerged at Puddleton-on-Sea, they certainly were rather a curious sight.

Evening had come by then and it was too dark to see anything but the long line of lights strung out like a necklace of bright beads along the esplanade. But there was a delicious smell of seaweed and the soft sound of the shush-shush-shushing of the waves chasing one another up the sand, and the hiss as they turned round and chased each other back again.

The children filed up at the station in an eager crocodile and marched the short distance to Great-Aunt Adelaide's hotel. This was very large and splendid, with lots of little towers and balconies and squirligigs like a gigantic cuckoo clock. Each child carried its possessions in a basketwork suit case. They were dressed in their white sailor suits (skirts for the girls) and round white sailor hats and I must say they looked extraordinarily silly; but these were their everyday summer clothes and there it was! Still, the sailor suits were complete with whistles on black cords, worn round their necks coming out from their big, square collars; and they thought that something could probably be made out of that. The Baby followed at the end of the crocodile, a bit weary after the long journey but stumping along gamely, its nappies coming down as usual. It had its whistle in its mouth and couldn't get it out because both its fat hands were occupied in lugging along its own little basket; and it certainly breathed rather curiously as it went.

Miss Prawn was on the steps of the hotel, holding out the chilblains in greeting, and Evangeline and Pug bouncing up and down with joy at sight of the army advancing out of the dark. I'm afraid the joy was not very sincere; as you know, the Brown children had stayed with Evangeline before. Sugar and Spice, the dachshunds, upon seeing Pug, ran up and nipped him smartly in the behind. Pug set up a shrill wow-wow-wowing, Evangeline threw herself with loud boo-hoos upon her dear Prawnie, Miss Prawn already was giving small, piercing cries of

despair at the realisation that the Brown children hadn't changed one bit – and now were here for the whole holiday. The children put their whistles to their lips and, blowing away merrily to conceal the uproar from Great-Aunt Adelaide, filed with pious faces into the hall. From the various hotel lounges appeared large, red, white-whiskered colonel-faces and large, angry old-lady-faces, in a state of considerable alarm. Great-Aunt Adelaide proceeded majestically down the stairs towards the children.

At sight of her, they hastily concealed their whistles in their mouths. 'How do you do, children,' said Aunt Adelaide with a stately bow; raising her lorgnette, however, to look with some anxiety into their faces which looked strangely puffed out (by the whistles) and, moreover, as though they had just passed through a black snowstorm. The children tried to reply, but all they could manage (on account of the whistles) was 'Whee-whee-whee-*wheeeeee*,' with a great deal of giggling. Nurse Matilda observed the giggling and banged quietly on the floor with her big black stick.

'You are tired and hungry,' said Aunt Adelaide, peering even more keenly into their train-smudged faces. 'You need a good supper and then up to bed. Chef has prepared a special meal for you.'

'Thick soup, steak and kidney puddings and plum duff,' said Miss Prawn, hopefully. I'm sorry to say that what she was hopeful about was that the children would all develop severe indigestion and spend the rest of the holiday in bed.

'How lovely!' the children tried to say; it was almost their favourite meal. But Nurse Matilda had banged with her big black stick and now the whistles were firmly stuck. 'Whee-*whee*-wheeee!' was all that came out, as they cast longing looks towards the big dining-room.

'Good heavens!' cried Aunt Adelaide, putting up the ear-trumpet. 'The journey has been too much for them altogether!' Even she could get the shrill whistling. 'Acute bronchitis. Up to bed with them immediately! Bread and milk,' she suggested to Nurse Matilda, imperiously, 'and plenty of any medicine you happen to have with you.' She shepherded Evangeline towards the dining-room door. 'Come, my dear, you will have to help eat up as much as possible of the treats prepared for the children. Three helpings of plum duff for *you*!' She looked over Evangeline, who strongly resembled a plum duff herself in her very dreadful dough-coloured dress with large dark spots. 'You could do with a little fattening up, dear child,' she said.

Whistling shrilly, the children marched sadly up to bed, got undressed, climbed in, sat up straight against the rather hard hotel pillows. 'Supper in a minute,' said Nurse Matilda, coming round with a huge bottle of very dreadful looking yellow mixture. 'Doses first. Open your mouths!'

The children shook their heads dumbly. At least you couldn't take doses with your mouth full of whistle. But Nurse Matilda banged once again with her big black stick . . .

After the doses came the bread and milk. Which was worse, it really was quite hard to tell. But when she had tucked them up and gone away for the night, the children said to one another (and they were no longer whistling): 'Didn't you think Nurse Matilda gave a little smile when she said good-night? Didn't you think she really looked – well, quite pretty?'

Except, they had to add, for that terrible sticking-out tooth.

And next morning – the sea! They rushed to the windows and looked out – and there it was: acres and acres of golden sand all washed by the waves, with little foamings of white at the edge of the water as though it hadn't quite got rid of the soap. And between the hotel and the sand, the broad esplanade with the bath-chair men already toiling off on their way to pick up their invalid old ladies and gentlemen and take them for rides along the promenade, like huge, disgruntled babies, sitting up in their prams. On the beach, the Punch and Judy man was putting up his striped canvas upright tent, with its high wooden ledge for Punch and Judy to fight on; the donkeys getting their grooming before the day's work began, giving children rides up and down the beach; a stout brown horse pulling the bathing machines down to the sea's edge so that respectable ladies could change inside and creep down the steps right into deep water, without any gentleman catching a glimpse of them in their bathing dresses – though the bathing dresses were made of good, thick material and came right up to their necks and right down to their ankles.

The children, as soon as breakfast was over, put on their own bathing dresses – which were very high and very long too, but covered with cheerful black and yellow stripes – and looking like a

horde of happy wasps, rushed down across the
sand and plunged into the water. Oh, how lovely
and roll-y and splashy and salty and tumble-y that
water felt! It bore them up as they floated,
frantically paddling with their front paws like
little dogs, it tumbled them head-over-heels back
to the shore, and sucked away the sand from
under them when they tried to stand up,
tumbling them back in again. The Baby had got a
strand of seaweed around its neck and was curled
up into a little round ball, tossing blissfully from
ripple to ripple, with its brown, shiny ribbons

streaming out behind it. I think it was the happiest hour they had ever had in their lives. Healthy and hearty, they trooped back to the hotel, and fortunately Evangeline hadn't been able to eat up all the steak-and-kidney pudding and plum duff, so Chef had heated up the rest for their lunch. Really, said the children among themselves, they could have a wonderful time here without even ever having to be naughty.

But I'm sure you will be sorry to hear that they *were* naughty; and the very next day. I suppose they had got into the habit of it and simply couldn't stop.

It was a lovely day, fair and unclouded and the sea very still. The children got up early and, in their wasp-bathing-dresses, crept down across the sands and into the water, went out as far as they could and, forming up into a long line, the baby bobbing at the end of it, swam up and down humping up their behinds and making a great deal of splashing. Soon all the elderly inhabitants of Puddleton were out on their balconies in their dressing-gowns, in a great state of excitement at seeing a black-and-yellow striped sea-monster of enormous length, lashing the waters in its rage and obviously looking about it for human prey. A message was sent to the coastguards who in turn sent messages to all the neighbouring seaside places, and soon vast crowds were advancing upon Puddleton-on-Sea. There was a dreadful row in the lifeboat station, little men, quite swallowed up in yellow macintoshes right up to their noses and yellow sou'westers right down to their chins, declaring in muffled voices that wrecks was one thing but dang them! if sea-monsters wasn't another. A great argument blew up, much complicated by the fact that owing to the high collars of the macintoshes and low brims of the sou'westers, no one could hear what anyone else was saying. By the time they had it all sorted out, the sea-monster had broken up into lots of boys and girls running about the beach, wrapped in towels to cover the black and yellow stripes. Clemency and Helen rushed up to the lifeboat men. 'One of our number is missing,' they cried, putting on very long, anxious faces; and added, 'The fattest.'

'Got by that theer monster!' cried the lifeboat men, going very pale.

'Dragged her down to the bottom of the sea,' suggested Nicholas. He explained: 'They bob up and down several times with their victims in their mouths, before they gobble them up.'

'You could drag her out of its jaws next time it comes bobbing up,' suggested Megan helpfully.

'Ow, dang!' said the lifeboat men, not at all charmed by this prospect. They looked round them for inspiration. 'Perhaps she just be 'oiding be' oind they rocks?'

'She couldn't,' said William. 'She couldn't find one large enough.' All the children began to run about, nevertheless, looking under heaps of stacked deck chairs, under the pier, round the bathing machines, earnestly looking for Evangeline, and bringing the lifeboat men's poor hearts still further down into their huge yellow boots with shrill cries of, 'No, she's not here! The monster must have got her! She'll have to be rescued!' And it was quite true that Evangeline was not there; she was humped up sound asleep in her warm hotel bed, making little snortling, snoring noises and one way and another not at all unlike a monster herself.

Nurse Matilda came down the hotel steps and

stood looking out at the beach. She saw the children running about the sands uttering cries of hideous foreboding, she saw the lifeboat men gloomily taking their boat down to the water's edge. They were carrying it upside down so that it looked like a large white beetle with lots of little yellow legs wavering about under it, bent at the knees and very much out of step; muffled cries of, 'Ow, dang!' echoed across the sand as, blinded by its depth, they banged and barged into obstacles which Justin and Louisa were busily putting in their way. Nurse Matilda lifted up her big black stick.

Half the children found themselves in the boat, squashed up between the lifeboat men and uttering a great many ow-dang's! of their own now, as each wave lifted the boat and rolled her this way and that and they all felt more and more sick. The lifeboat men had suddenly become very brave and kept shouting 'Dar she be!' and 'Monster a-hoy!' and rowing off in all directions, only pausing to cry, 'Lean over the side, young master, there, that's roight!' The children tried to explain that there had been no sea-monster really but they seemed to feel too sick to utter; and now lifeboats began appearing from all the other stations and soon there was a positive little regatta of them, and the water echoed with cries of 'Dang!' and 'Dar she blows!' and 'She'll be 'oiding in that there rough water over there, make for the

breakers!' The children leaned over the side and, silently heaving, longed for the shore . . .

But ashore, the rest of them were still searching. They searched and they searched. They knew that Evangeline wasn't lost, but Nurse Matilda had banged with her big black stick, and they had to go on looking for her. The heaps of stacked deck chairs nipped their fingers, the sharp rocks scratched their bare toes, the tall metal struts under the pier were slimy with seaweed, the waves came whishing in and swept their feet from under them so that they sat down abruptly in pools of chilly water – but they had to go on clambering about, idiotically calling out for Evangeline. Miss Prawn came out on to the esplanade and ran up and down with plaintive bleats of terror, her chilblains clasped to her flat bosom. Pug followed her faithfully and Sugar and Spice faithfully followed Pug. 'Wow, dang!' yapped Pug, as nip-nip went Sugar and Spice at his behind; or at any rate, it sounded very much like it. The children toiled on.

The Baby toiled with them. Up and down the beach it tottered, its nappies coming down as usual, its little pink starfish hands held out anxiously before it, cries of 'Egangekeeng!' and 'Cay peag!' rending the air. 'Oh, yes,' said the children; and, 'Please!' they all begged Nurse Matilda, standing round her in an imploring circle; but for once even this magic word made no difference and on and on they went . . .

In her hotel bedroom, Evangeline heard the cries in her sleep and, like some monster indeed, stirring in the deeps, humphed herself out of bed, put on one of her very ghastly dresses, of purple with crimson blotches, most suitable for a sunny day at the sea, stumped downstairs to join dear Prawnie for some Healthful Fresh Air before breakfast. So dense was the crowd on the esplanade, hoping like anything to see the monster coming up, dripping, with a fat little girl in its mouth, that even Evangeline in the dress escaped notice; and hearing a small, piping cry of 'Egangekeeng!' she stepped up to the Baby and said, innocently: 'Yes?'

'Egangekeeng!' cried the Baby and jumped so hard for joy that its nappies really did come right down and lay in a round white nest, with its fat little feet in the middle like two pink eggs. It hauled the nappies up hastily, blushing a little all over its sweet, round face and, holding the nappies up with one hand, tugged Evangeline with the other to Nurse Matilda. 'I koung Egangekeeng, I koung Egangekeeng!' it cried, joyfully presenting its prize who stood like a stout purple cow, staring stupidly at the commotion around her. The children all came and gathered about them. 'So, Nurse Matilda, can we stop searching now?'

'Certainly not,' said Nurse Matilda. 'You have given a great deal of trouble, severely frightened a good many people and spoilt a lovely sunny morning for everyone. You had better go on as you chose to begin.'

This was dreadful. They saw themselves spending the whole of the rest of their holiday – the whole of the rest of their *lives* – beach-combing for Evangeline; looking more and more curious as they got older and older, so that at last no one would have anything to do with them and they must live on limpets and seaweed, curled up at nights beneath the dank pier, in their black and yellow bathing dresses like a little swarm of sodden bees. They cried out piteously: 'Oh, Nurse Matilda—!'

The baby looked up into her face and its big blue eyes filled with tears. 'But I *koung* her,' it protested.

'Oh, Nurse Matilda,' said the children. 'The poor Baby! It's so proud of having found her. At least let the Baby stop!'

Nurse Matilda stooped down and picked up the Baby and held it warm and safe against her shoulder. 'Ah!' she said. 'That's the first thing you've done today that hasn't been selfish and unkind.' And just for a moment, there came round her, her little golden glow: and in that one moment the seas were empty, the crowds had gone and the Brown family was sitting down comfortably to breakfast.

But up at the lifeboat station, the little yellow men, dressed up in their tarpaulins and sou'-westers, all ready for a wreck, were shaking their heads in amazement . . . 'Dang me if Oi didn't have a strange dream laast noight,' they were saying to one another . . .

Chapter 5

THAT day, after lunch, the children were sent off for a walk. 'I have allowed Miss Prawn to bring her mother with her for the holiday,' said Aunt Adelaide. 'You can all take turns in pushing her along the promenade, in her bath-chair.' Miss Prawn's mother was a very dreadful old lady. She had once had a deep passion for cheese but the children had sent her a bar of soap instead and now she much preferred that and as a result was in a constant state of lather. As she had just had a substantial meal, her bath-chair soon became almost invisible in clouds of foam. The Baby, stumping along in the rear of the crocodile, kept getting swept into it, disappearing from sight for a while and emerging, all smiles, with its nappies coming down as usual.

Other old ladies and gentlemen stopped to stare. 'Beaten white of egg,' explained the children. 'A new treatment. Takes years off your age!' The old ladies and gentlemen set up a great hullabalooing because *they* couldn't be covered in beaten white of egg too. Their bath-chair men gathered round them in heated argument, Miss Prawn joined them full of anxious denials. The children, while her back was turned, quickly swapped two bath-chairs and they set off once more; now wheeling a stout gentleman, very happy in the belief that he had suddenly been covered in white of egg and would emerge from the foam practically a schoolboy again. In fact he emerged still a stout old man, covered up in rugs – to the dreadful dismay of Miss Prawn who thought the whole thing had been too much for her mother, who had suddenly blown up very big and red, and grown a large white moustache. The children proceeded meekly on their way. They had found a live jelly-fish and contrived to place it on top of Evangeline's head, where it lay very dank and quivery, its tentacles constantly falling over her eyes and being brushed aside with loud appeals to Prawnie because her hair seemed to have got all wet. Miss Prawn, however, had decided that the moustache must just be soap-suds and was trying to scrape it off, to the great rage of the old gentleman – even her Mama's voice appeared to have taken a turn for the worse; and for once she was deaf to Evangeline's appeals. 'Oh, Evangeline, it's not only your hair, the whole top of your head seems to have gone all soft!' cried the children, helpfully. Evangeline

put up her hand, felt only cold, wet jelly and bolted for home. Pug followed her, yapping at her heels, and Sugar and Spice followed close behind him, nipping away.

The children marched serenely on, pausing only for Camilla and Jocelyn to give a slight twist to the sign at the crossroads, which said on one arm TO LITTLE PIDDLINGTON and on the other TO PUDDLETON-ON-SEA. On the way back, they passed a large nursing home where a desperate scene was in progress because the bath-chair man who had wheeled away a stout, red-faced old gentleman with a large white moustache, had returned with a thin, pale old lady, loudly demanding tea and a bar of Sunlight Soap. The Browns took no notice but filed innocently by. At Ocean View and Sandybanks and the Bay Hotel, landladies were having heated arguments with total strangers who, thanks to the sign-post, were under the impression that they had safely arrived in Little Piddlington, and now, declaring that they had booked rooms in advance, were angrily forcing their way in, children, luggage, dogs and all. No doubt in the real Little Piddlington, scenes of the same nature were going on. Ocean View and Sandybanks being next door to one another, Danny and Joel were able, while the people were indoors quarrelling, to mix up all the luggage so that nobody knew whose was whose, and there soon followed a tremendous uproar, sorting that out too. Farther down the road, Hilary and

Quentin had unscrewed the sign from a gate saying, in ornamental letters, HAPPY-HOLME BOARDING HOUSE and exchanged it with the one next door saying LIBERTY HALL, which, as the guests were to discover, was not the same thing at *all*.

The junior boys of a local school filed by in a crocodile of pairs, following their master, all dressed (except for the master, who I must say would have looked even sillier) in the regulation white summer sailor suits. The younger boys of the Brown family, similarly attired, immediately attached themselves to the end of the queue and marched along with them, throwing their arms back and forth with a martial swing, heads held high – to the great bewilderment of the master who, having started out with a dozen boys, now found himself with about thirty. 'Spots before the eyes,' he kept saying to himself, counting the boys over and over again. 'It was that lobster for lunch.' The boys seemed badly out of step and he cried out, 'Left – *right*! Left – *right*!' in a sergeant-major voice. The boys from the school did a little skip to get back into step and the Browns at once did a little skip to get them out again. At the entrance to their hotel, they peeled silently off from the end of the crocodile, leaving the master more mystified than ever. 'Spots before the eyes is one thing,' he wrote earnestly home to his mother that evening, 'but boys before the eyes is another. And this morning, I thought I saw more boys than were really there. I shan't eat lobster again.' And poor man – he did love it! It was rather a shame.

The children went quietly into the dining-room and sat down in fours and sixes at the little hotel tables. The old ladies and gentlemen looked tenderly into their innocent, radiant faces and said to each other that it was pleasant to have the place enlivened by a little sprinkling of Youth. The sprinkling was in fact rather a heavy shower but they hadn't come to realise that yet; and they watched with enthusiasm the way the children, who appeared to have rescued a large and quivering jelly-fish from some situation of peril, carried it lovingly down to the sea and set it free.

Between tea time and supper the children were very busy:

Francesca and Teresa had let out the seams of some of Evangeline's dresses and taken in the seams of some of the others; and Aunt Adelaide and Miss Prawn were in a terrible taking because the poor child seemed to be changing so rapidly from fat to thin.

Matthew had put fruit salts in the sugar sifter and everybody's pudding was beginning to fizzle, and –

Lucy had written with a soft pencil on top of the bald patch of the head waiter YOU ARE ALL SILLY OLD FOOLS; and every time he turned his back on anyone, they rose up in great wrath and gave notice.

All the other children were doing simply dreadful things too.

And so the days went sunnily by. The skies were as blue as the sea and the sea was as blue as the sky and all glittery with dancing points of light. The sand was golden and smooth, with only some hard, damp wrinkles where the tide had turned and gone out again. Along the water's edge stood the bathing machines all day, in a long row. They were like little gypsy caravans and each morning a stout brown horse with wet brown legs, towed them down into the water, led by a stout old woman with wet *red* legs, who unharnessed him there and took him back for another one. The ladies from the hotels hurried

across the beach in their nice, dark serge summer dresses with their large hats and parasols, climbed up the steps and dived behind a thick curtain, each into her own little caravan; and, clad in a dark serge bathing dress which began at her neck and ended in long frilled drawers down to her ankles, her head covered in a huge frilled cap, crept coyly down the steps on the side that led into the water. The bathing machines, as we know, were pulled in so far, that the water was deep enough to cover them up to their necks the moment they got into it: so that nothing so dreadful could happen as a gentleman catching even a glimpse of the long serge drawers. In the water they bobbed up and down, often holding on for safety to the lady with the wet red legs, and uttering shrill screams of what the children supposed must be delight, before hurrying up the steps into their caravans again.

The children had a splendid time diving in under the machines and banging smartly on the underneaths of their floors (so that the poor ladies thought there might be gentlemen hiding there spying upon the moment when they should descend into the sea): or tugging away at the wheels pushing the bathing machines higher up the beach, so that the bathers had to come right up out of the water to climb back in: goodness, if a gentlemen had seen them *then*! (Actually, the gentlemen were quite safe, on a decently distant part of the beach, also covered from head to foot in solid bathing dresses, mostly striped, splashing about in manly fashion, and dashing modestly back across the sand to change behind the rocks. The children contented themselves with switching the little heaps of clothes left beneath the various rocks, so that there was a fine old scrummage, stout elderly parties trying to struggle into bright club blazers many sizes too small for them, smart young blades clapping on straw hats and finding themselves suddenly blind and deaf.)

The little donkeys chiff-chuffed through the sand giving children rides, and the Brown children spent all their pocket-money buying rides and not having them, so that the donkeys could rest. They got Pug into a frill and put him up on the ledge of the Punch and Judy booth, to the great rage of Pug and alarm of the Punch and Judy man, who thought his Toby had suddenly had his long, thin terrier nose flattened in; and to the great delight of the real Toby who had a splendid time, running about playing with Sugar and Spice – rushing into the sea and rushing straight out again to shake themselves all over whoever happened to be near them. I must confess that Sugar and Spice were not the most popular dogs on the beach, that sunny summer at Puddleton-on-Sea.

And I'm afraid the Browns weren't the most popular children.

Chapter 6

ND so, as I say, the days passed; till one afternoon Great-Aunt Adelaide announced that she would give a picnic party on the beach.

Great-Aunt Adelaide's idea of a picnic was to arrange a large ring of deck chairs on the sand, as close to the hotel as possible, and invite all the more old and ferocious ladies of the hotel as her guests; with her own maid, Fiddle, to wait upon the company. The children spent a busy morning in preparation for this treat, and this is what they were doing:

Sally and Adam were glue-ing together the wooden struts of one of the deck chairs.

Cecily and Roland were making small slits across the seats.

Marcus and Camilla were boring three narrow passages through the sand, leading to the middle of

*where the tablecloth would be spread; and starting off
a crab at each entrance.*

*Felicity and Lucy were collecting bits of foam from
the sea and forming it into little balls which really
did make the most life-like meringues.*

*Almond and Theodora were lining the sand-wiches
with seaweed.*

*Mary was filling up the sugar bowls with nice, white
sand, and—*

*Sarah Jane and Alexander had borrowed a
performing seal from the aquarium (without asking
the keeper's permission) and seated him, wrapped in
a rug from the waist downward, in one of the deck
chairs; and painted a white collar round his neck.*

*All the other children were doing simply dreadful
things too.*

The ladies assembled in stout cloth dresses with
stout linen petticoats over several stout *flannel*
petticoats, and wearing large hats covered with
feathers and flowers – evidently their idea of
comfortable wear for a boiling hot day at the
seaside. Evangeline was adorned in one of her
more hideous garments, mustard yellow splodged
quite horribly with a sickly green; with a floppy
hat which fell down all round her fat red face,

most mercifully concealing it from the beholders. Fiddle hovered anxiously outside the circle, waiting to hand cups and plates. The children had filled her shoes with the real meringues and little clouds of white puffed up round her ankles with every step; the cream had sunk down to the bottom and made a very satisfying squlidge, squlidge as she trudged wretchedly about in the sand.

The ladies assembled with joyful cries of admiration at the feast laid out on the white tablecloth at their feet. One sponge cake was missing, which Rhiannon had thoughtfully removed in advance and was now quietly crumbling on top of the large flowered hats. There was a fearful struggle with Miss Prawn's deck chair, which refused to open. Evangeline rushed to her dear Prawnie's assistance and they emerged at last, their hands full of broken wood, wrapped in the red and white striped canvas, like two pale prunes in a slice of streaky bacon. The rest of the guests were settling down happily, all unaware that beneath them the little slits in the canvas were beginning slowly to get larger. 'But who is the very dark gentleman with the moustaches?' they murmured admiringly to Great-Aunt Adelaide. 'Pray present us!'

The dark gentleman presented himself, in a growly voice which appeared to come from very deep down — almost from underneath his deck chair, one might have said. 'Reverend George Tomlinson-Seal, dear ladies,' he replied 'Retired missionary from Mmmmmglummmba-Mmmmmglummmba. You will pardon my not rising to salute you. I have unfortunately lost my legs.'

'What, both of them?' cried the ladies, perturbed; and it did sound rather careless.

'Sacrifice to my parishioners,' said the reverend gentleman. 'My dear Mmmmm-glummmba-Mmmmmglummmbans.' A very special feast, he explained. One could hardly offer less.

'A feast?' cried the ladies, growing rather pale.

'Ah, well, one was younger then. I daresay,' said the Reverend, with jocular modesty, 'that I'd prove a rather tougher dish nowadays!'

'*Dish?*'

'Cannibals to a man, dear fellows!' From beneath the deck chair came a loud smacking of lips. 'And one really couldn't blame them. A nice plump young girl, for example – one does get a taste for it.' He looked round the laden tablecloth. 'Those sandwiches – not by any chance –?'

'Fiddle!' said Aunt Adelaide, sharply commanding. Fiddle, lint white in the face, squidged through the sand with the plate, snatching back her arm in great haste as the guest reached out for a sandwich. With one large hand which, despite the heat of the day, appeared to be clad in a rather damp dark fur glove, he picked one up and thrust it, whole, into his mouth. 'Only strawberry jam,' said the growly voice, disappointed. 'I had for a moment hoped . . . And I *prefer* it raw . . .' The faint squeals of the ladies prevented any further confessions. He rose rather rockily to his feet. 'I had better get back to my lodgings. They understand my requirements there. Perhaps one or two of these dear children would come with me?' He looked rather longingly at the stout figure of Evangeline.

Miss Prawn flung herself in front of Evangeline with outspread arms, ready to defend her to the last crumb. Sarah Jane and Alexander each took a flipper – I mean an arm – of the unwelcome guest and, still wrapped in the rug, he unsteadily departed.

The keeper was much surprised to see one of his seals being supported back into the aquarium by two kind children with innocent looks on their faces. He now wore no rug but appeared to have a white band painted round his neck, and to

have been eating strawberry jam. 'You never know what these varmints'll get up to,' said the keeper, giving the seal a playful shove to get it back into the pool and reaching for a bucket of fish. Unfortunately he was somewhat short of sight and Sarah Jane and Alexander had to catch most of the fish and pass it on, the seal applauding with a great clapping of flippers, licking his lips at the delicious mixture of raw fish and strawberry jam. The children wiped the fish off their hands down the sides of their clothes and went back to the picnic party. 'Goodness,' they cried, 'you should see his landlady's children!' Not one of them still complete, they said, with all its limbs; but no-body seemed to mind a bit, they were all delighted to give an arm here, a leg there, to keep Mr. Tomlinson-Seal happy and at home, so far from his dear Mmmmmglummmba-Mmmmm-glummmbans. And indeed you could see how glad he was to be back with the family; he was evidently devoted to children. 'He loved *you*,' they said, meaningfully to Evangeline; and added, in great consternation: 'Why has Miss Prawn fainted away? He only likes *fat* people.'

The ladies had not been having the happiest of times. When they took sips of tea, the sand-sugar filled their mouths uncomfortably with grit; after Mr Seal's visit they no longer cared much for red jam sandwiches and jelly, and when they reached for a lovely fluffy white meringue, it was only sea-foam and their teeth met the middle with a jolting click. If they had any left, that is; for the seaweed sandwiches had proved the greatest success of all, the ladies' teeth becoming clamped on the seaweed and coming away with it: so that they sat chumbling angrily on their poor gums, while their teeth remained, grinning back at them rather dreadfully, fixed into the sandwiches in their hands. And when they might have turned to a nice, soft, chumbley sponge cake – the sponge cake seemed to have disappeared . . .

The sponge cake, as we know, had been crumbled by Rhiannon into the crowns of the ladies' large hats.

It was a beautiful day. In the golden dazzle of the sunshine, the sky was all hazily blue, the sea sparkled as though it had been sprinkled with diamonds, its white fingers tickling their way up the beach and hastily scuttling back, with a little sighing sound, as though it were playing a game, trying to see how far it could creep up to the people's bare toes before anyone noticed it . . . All around them were other picnic parties, children with buckets and spades, children playing cricket, children paddling at the water's edge, holding the hands of mothers and fathers with bunched-up skirts and rolled-up trouser legs. Heads bobbed in the water, nannies were drying their charges, wrapped up in enormous striped beach towels, rubbing away so vigorously that the poor little heads rolled helplessly, hair flopping, on the slender necks. Whole families were earnestly building sand-castles, tunnelling tiny arches and door-ways which collapsed slowly inwards as the damp sand dried out in the sun. Above it all, the seagulls called shrilly, wheeling, drifting, suddenly swooping down . . .

It wasn't long before their beady eyes spotted the bits of cake which Rhiannon had dropped into the ladies' hats.

The ladies, being friends of Great-Aunt Adelaide, were, as we've said, mostly very large and rather fierce. There was an angry, stout old party called Mrs Grobble and another very angry stout old party called Mrs Rumbletum and a simply furious stout old party with a strong foreign accent, called Mrs Guttziz; and there was also poor Miss Fizzle who had come down here to convalesce. You remember Miss Fizzle? – the children had changed over the charts at the hospital and her temperature seemed to have shot up suddenly from normal to a hundred and four. She had never quite got over it and now she went quite pale when a seagull dived down and seized a bit of cake from the crown of her hat. 'Eaouw! Eaouw!' cried Miss Fizzle in ladylike accents, and 'Ow, ow!' cried all the other ladies and 'Owchn, Owchn!' cried Mrs Guttziz as peck, peck, peck went the hard beaks banging away for crumbs, at the tops of their heads.

But soon the last morsel was gone and there came little tearing sounds, as bits of ribbon and

feather and lace began to go too, not to mention large lumps of imitation flowers and fruit, from the hats themselves; and at last – a whole hat. 'Oh, Mrs Grobble, look at your bald head!' cried the children, helpfully, and, 'Ow, ow, my hat!' cried Mrs Grobble, scarlet in the face with outraged dismay.

'We'll get it for you,' cried the children and off they went. 'A comet, a comet!' they declaimed, dashing about the beach in little doomladen groups. 'A comet descending! The end of the world has come!' The people looked up and saw a bright object sailing above them, with long strands streaming behind it of Mrs Grobble's rich brown hair, and they snatched up their children, spades, buckets and all and made tracks for home. The seagull, disturbed by the fuss, flew out to sea and dropped the hat. 'An octopus! An octopus!' screamed the children, deserting the beach to flock down to the water's edge. 'Swim for it! You'll all be seized and dragged down to the bottom of the sea!' And indeed a very dreadful creature it looked, bright blue and pink, covered with large irregular lumps of what had once been artificial roses, and trailing its rippling tentacles of net and hair. The bathers took one look at it and struck out for the shore.

Back at the picnic, Mrs Grobble sat almost bursting with rage and mortification, looking like a monster Easter egg, crimson in the face right up to her forehead, where the colour suddenly stopped, leaving a bald white dome. The hat was washed gently in to the edge of the beach and the children rescued it and helpfully slapped it back on to her head. They had got it wrong way round and she sat looking very balefully out at them from behind the long strands of dripping wet hair. But after all, they were only being kind to her – weren't they?

Two other seagulls had meanwhile seized Mrs Guttziz's hat and Mrs Rumbletum's but, scared by all the noise, soon dropped them and flew off. Unfortunately the hats fell back on to the wrong heads. Mrs Guttziz peered through her lorgnette at Mrs Rumbletum, who now wore an enormous confection of orange and pink which sat very oddly above her rather purple face. 'Mrs Rumpletoom – I haf not perfore opserfing that we are wearing the same hetz!'

'Why, no indeed,' said Mrs Rumbletum,

recognising her own hat on Mrs Guttziz's head.

'A ferry hendsome het. Extra-ortinary,' said Mrs Guttziz, looking at *her* hat on Mrs Rumbletum's head, 'thet we shoult buyink both the same.' She added with charming frankness that on Mrs Rumbletum's part, it had been a great mistake. 'Your complexion iss not gutt. Qvuite wronk to choosing oranche for colour off a het.'

'My hat is pale blue,' said Mrs Rumbletum, gazing at it as it sat perched on top of Mrs Guttziz.

'Oranche,' said Mrs Guttziz, gazing back at her own hat, on Mrs Rumbletum. She appealed to the other ladies who up to now had been riveted (rather joyfully I'm afraid) upon Mrs Grobble's misadventures, with her own octopus hat. 'What colour would you sayink iss Mrs Rumpletoom's het?'

'Orange,' said the ladies, a trifle astonished at finding Mrs Rumbletum's large purple face now crowned as with fire; but not yet able to collect their wits.

'Oranche,' said Mrs Guttziz, triumphantly. But she peered still more closely through her glasses at Mrs Rumbletum and suddenly let out a loud bellow of alarm. 'Move beck! Be careful! She iss goink out of her mindt!'

'What's the matter?' cried all the ladies, driving the hind feet of their deck chairs deeper and deeper back into the sand, as they tried to move away from the dangerous Mrs Rumbletum.

'The seagulse hes pecked too hardt on her head and this hes affected her mindt. Yellow hair,' said Mrs Guttziz, firmly reminding them. 'From out a bottle, perheps, I am not sayink: but yellow. Ant now – look et it! You are hearink of people goink grey in one night. In fife min'yutes, Mrs Rumpletoom is goink white as snow.' Mrs Guttziz's own hair was as white as snow, but most of it had come away, speared with two large hatpins to her hat, which now, of course, hair and all, sat upon Mrs Rumbletum's head.

Mrs Rumbletum had had an unhappy afternoon. She had been much shaken by the cannibal revelations of the Reverend Tomlinson-Seal, then at finding her gums clashing together as her teeth were carried away, fixed into a seaweed sandwich held in her hand. There were still remnants in her mouth of mixed sand–sugar and sea-foam; and suddenly for a moment she had felt her head go very light and air-y, only a moment later to become as though a heavy weight lay upon it. Now all the ladies were staring at her, open-mouthed, assuring her that her pale blue hat was bright orange and her golden hair was white. (It was true that Mrs Rumbletum's gold came out of a bottle; but at least her hair belonged to her head; only now it was covered with Mrs Guttziz's white hair, complete with the orange hat.) She rose to her feet, trembling all over like a great blackcurrant jelly, crowned with gold. 'Yes,' she said simply. 'I am going mad.' And she crossed her wrists dramatically before her, as though ready for the strait-jacket. 'Take me away!'

The children, delighted to do so, clustered round to lead her off as she seemed to be so anxious to go; but suddenly . . .

Suddenly everything seemed to happen at once. The crabs had long ago started down the three little passages which Marcus and Camilla had tunnelled, leading to the middle of the picnic tablecloth. Sugar and Spice and Pug, sniffing happily round, had discovered the entrances and each chosen one and started tunnelling in on his own. Unfortunately, at the end of each, was sitting very contentedly under the tablecloth a large live crab. Nip, nip, nip went the crabs, confronted by three moist black noses; and Wow, wow, wow! went Sugar and Spice and Pug, trying to back away; and 'Ow, ow, ow!' cried the ladies in dreadful alarm as the whole picnic suddenly seemed to come alive. Cups and saucers flew up

in the air and came down with a crash, cakes and sandwiches flung themselves about as though the beach had erupted beneath them, the teapot shot up and streamed hot brown tea, the milk jugs shot up and streamed cold white milk, the foam meringues wafted about like little clouds, the seaweed sandwiches split wide and showed their glossy brown. There was a tremendous ow-ow-owing as the ladies struggled to their feet and fled in a panic stricken rout, streaking out across the sand to the safety of the hotel, led by Great Aunt Adelaide Stitch, fearfully hooting through her high, rhinoceros-horn nose.

Soon the whole beach was in confusion. The stout button-boots of the ladies crashed in mad stampede through the parties of picnickers, games of cricket, circles of aunties and mums, gossiping over their knitting, sitting round on their little striped camp stools, happy though hot. Mrs Grobble had got one foot stuck in a child's tin bucket and made a terrible clanking as she pounded along, Mrs Rumbletum had snatched up a wooden spade and threshed about, clearing her formidable path. Clouds of crushed meringue flew up about Fiddle's lean legs as she squelched through the sand, still clutching a teapot and dreadfully dribbling hot brown tea as she ran. Poor Prawnie, blinded by lather, was madly pushing her mother's bath chair this way and that, zooming up a rock with it, down the other side – feet hardly touching the ground – galloping across sand-castles to the cries of outraged children, driving her wild way slap over the tummies of furious old gentlemen, sleeping on the sand with newspapers spread over their faces . . . Sugar and Spice and Pug had emerged and shaken off their crabs, and now fled about through the confusion, hysterically barking; the crabs scuttled down to the sea again, nipping right, left and centre as they went. Through it all, the children ran crying, 'A volcano! It's erupting! Fly for your lives . . .!' And at last, as the beach emptied and they found themselves alone, collapsed into the deck chairs round the wreck of Great-Aunt Adelaide's picnic, and lay there, speechless with laughter.

Nurse Matilda stood on the edge of the promenade and looked down on them; and lifted up her big black stick . . .

And the little slits in the canvas began to grow. They grew and they grew; and the children slowly sank down and down till their bottoms touched the sand and their knees were tight up under their chins. And there they all stayed.

From the esplanade above them, came the clamour of children screaming for abandoned buckets and spades, of families sorting themselves out from other families – many were so plastered with sand as to be unrecognisable; of nannies giving notice, of hotel guests packing up and departing for ever; or departing for ever, with*out* packing up, in terror of the volcano. But as time went by, the sounds grew less and less and at last silence fell. The hot day cooled, a little breeze came from over the waters, carrying with it the briny scent of the sea; the tide crept in, smoothing out with its white fingers of foam, the poor, torn-up, tumbled sand – and softly crept out again. The sun went down. The evening came.

Curled up tight with their chins on their knees – the children cried out: 'Oh, Nurse Matilda,

please help us! Please let us go!' But all was silent and quiet. No answer came.

And night fell and the moon rose and in its light the sea lay like wrinkled black treacle; and there was no sound but the sh–sh–sh of the waves, murmuring a lullaby to all the living things in the deeps of the ocean.

Murmuring a lullaby . . . The children's eyes stared up, unblinking, at the winking stars. They longed and longed for sleep – but they were wide awake. The sea was singing its lullaby to them but they were caught there, fastened for ever and ever, and could not even go to sleep. They rocked and wriggled in the fast clasp of the wooden arms of the deck chairs. 'If only we could get free!' they said. 'If only we could get free, we'd run away. It's horrible here at the seaside, we could run away and go back to our own dear home . . .' But they couldn't get free; the deck chairs held them tight.

And suddenly a voice said: 'Where's the Baby?' and another voice said, with a shake in it, 'Yes, what's happened to the Baby?' and another voice said with a break in it, 'With all the rushing about and laughing and having fun, we forgot all about the Baby . . .' And another voice said with tears in it: 'We've been selfish, and beastly, making things horrid for other people and spoiling their day; and not even given a thought to our own poor Baby . . .'

And Nurse Matilda stood up there on the promenade with the drowsy baby held safe against her shoulder, and looked down at them and listened: and smiled. And if the children could have seen her face in the moonlight, I think they would have said: 'All of a sudden – doesn't she look *beautiful?*'

If only it hadn't been for that one huge tooth sticking straight out over her lower lip.

Nurse Matilda lifted up her big black stick and brought it down – but very gently. And the tight wooden deck chairs released their hold and the moon drew a veil of cloud across her bright face, so that all was dark and quiet; and the sea sang its murmurous lullaby; and the children's eyes closed – and they were fast asleep.

Fast asleep – and dreaming.

Chapter 7

THE children were dreaming. They dreamed that the deck chairs released their hold; and they all leapt to their feet and cried: 'We'll run away! Let's run away! Let's run home!' And they began to run.

They ran and they ran. The moon had drawn aside her veiling of cloud and shone down brightly on the wrinkled black sea, and the blurred white sand. Along the beach, they went – scattering the ruins of sand-castles, hopping over crumpled tin buckets and broken wooden spades, crashing through abandoned picnics, skipping over deck chairs trampled into match-wood in the panic stampede after the eruption of the volcano beneath their own picnic. They ran and they ran. Hopping over more spades and buckets, more picnics, more smashed-up deck chairs – and more of them and more of them and more . . . The beach seemed very long and when Puddleton-on-Sea was left far behind them, still the sand stretched on ahead. And, it was very awkward, but as they ran, little stinging puffs of crushed white sugar seemed to be rising in clouds about their ankles, and squlidge, squlidge went their feet, sucking in and out of their shoes as though they had been filled with whipped cream. The Big Ones were in the lead, the Middling Ones following, the Little Ones helping the Tinies, trailing behind. In the rear came Pug with his round, pale brown behind and his stump of tail; and nip, nip, nip went Sugar and Spice, following Pug; and nip, nip, nip went three large, angry crabs, following Sugar and Spice. 'Wow wow wow!' went Pug and 'Wow wow wow!' went Sugar and Spice and nip, nip, nip went the crabs; and, 'Oh, dear,' cried the Little Ones, passing it along the line, up to the Middling Ones and so on up to the Big Ones in the lead, 'we're so tired. Can't we stop running, just for a minute?'

But somehow they couldn't stop running. They had to go on.

They ran and they ran. Miss Prawn appeared

from nowhere, belting along beside them, her chilblains glowing rosily through the white foam as she propelled her mother's bath-chair. The old lady sat very contentedly, munching at a bar of soap. It made the children hungry, just to hear her jaws snap on each new bite. 'Couldn't you spare us just a crumb?' they begged. 'But it's soap,' said a disembodied voice from deep within the foam. 'Why must she always eat soap?' cried the children, resentfully, jogging on. 'Well, it *is a bath-chair*,' said Miss Prawn loyally, jogging too.

They ran and they ran. And now all the cream

had gone and their shoes were filled with little icicles and their feet were getting very cold, and yet at the same time their heads were getting very hot and they realised that, his stout form wobbling like a jelly as he went, Podge Green was lollopping along beside them. 'Don't come near us, don't come near us,' cried the children, 'you'll give us your cold!' But they realised that what they really were saying was 'Dote cub dear us, dote cub dear us,' and they'd got it already. Still, that did seem to settle it. 'We're ill,' they cried. 'We've got codes id our doses, we bust go idto hospidal!' And sure enough, up rushed a fleet of little men, bearing stretchers, all at the ready. But just as they were about to stop the children running by sheer force, and strap them on to the stretchers (still feebly kicking, no doubt, but covered with nice red blankets to tuck them in) Sir Minsupp Izgizzard appeared, holding up a commanding hand. 'Women and horses first!' he cried, and up out of the sea came a horde of stout little old women with wet red legs, each leading a stout horse with wet *brown* legs – and the ambulance men set upon *them* instead, and soon had them all comfortably settled on the stretchers. With a ringing of bells and stamping of hooves, a fleet of horse-drawn ambulances came dashing across the sand and, already neighing away in a very showing-off manner about their operations, the stout brown-legged horses were carried off, with the stout red-legged ladies in their wake. The children ran on and now they turned and spun in dizzy little circles as they ran. 'It's too buch,' they cried. 'We've got codes, we're ill, we're dyig, we cad't go od.' But they had to, just the same.

But salvation was in sight; for there ahead of them stood Mr Privy, the Vicar, and surely he must love his neighbours and stop them running if he could. He looked rather odd, his neat suit of clerical grey being crowned by a small black velvet nightcap; but the children were thankful to see him, nightcap and all. They set up a little song, managing as well as they could, considering their colds. 'People who are kide ad beek, Bister Privy,' sang the children, 'Ad always turd the other cheek, Will fill their lives with berry fud, Bister Privy, Ad be belov'd by everywud,' and they jogged up and down, marking time and confidently waiting for Mr Privy to turn the other cheek and become lovable. But Mr Privy only burst into a hymn of his own. 'On-ward Christ-yun so-ho-hol-diers,' sang Mr Privy, and instead of turning his cheek, held out his hand and warmly shook each of theirs as they passed by . . .

And as they passed by again . . . And as they passed by *again* . . . For now the children found themselves running round and round in a circle, shaking hands with Mr Privy, and running on round. And it seemed that this might have gone on for ever, if there had not appeared across the face of the moon a dark veil which resolved itself into a swarm of bees. 'Rud for it, rud for it, Bister Privy!' cried the children, rudding for it thebselves — I mean running for it themselves. 'There's a swarb of bees.' '*I*'b dot frighted of bees,' said Mr Privy (for even he seemed to have caught the infection), and remained where he was with out-stretched hand and a pleasant word ready for each comer. 'But they're dot bees after all,' cried the children. 'Look, look!' — and indeed the bees had all clustered together now, and they saw that the swarm was really a sea-monster, striped yellow and black, which had risen up out of the water and was making for them with a very determined look upon its terrifying face. 'A bodster, bodster!' cried the children running harder than ever; at least not in circles now, however, but streaking out across the sand, led by Mr Privy and with Miss Prawn at full pelt by their side; only her mother sitting chumping away happily, quite safe within her blanket of white. Sugar and Spice and Pug brought up the rear with the three crabs still going nip, nip, nip behind.

Or rather the *two* crabs: for the sea-monster had closed upon them now and reached out a great curled, flaming tongue and golloped up the last in the line . . . And the second last . . . And the third last . . . And now its hot breath was singe-ing the ends of the dachshunds' tails. 'Wow, wow, wow!' cried Sugar and Spice and 'Ow, ow, ow!' cried the children. 'Save us, help us, we're all going to be gobbled up . . .!'

There came no answer – only the gentle shush-shush of the sea, singing its lullaby. But the shush-shush seemed to grow louder and become a plash-plash – the plash-plash of oars; and through the plash-plash of the oars came muffled cries of

'Ow, dang!' and 'Dar she blows!' and there was the crumbling sound of a lifeboat's keel running up on to the sand, and out of the lifeboat tumbled a horde of little men in yellow macs, running this way and that, their heads tilted well back to avoid being totally blinded by their huge yellow sou' – westers. 'Dar she be!' they cried, their voices muffled in yellow macintosh. 'Monster a-hoy!' 'Yes, it *is* a-hoy!' cried the children. 'It's a-hoying along behind us like anything, we'll soon all be gobbled up.' '*We*'ll save ye, *we*'ll save ye!' cried the little men and went dashing off back to the boat. 'Where be bait?' They evidently couldn't find the bait (though when they finally did, it was large enough) – and there were great cries of 'Ow, dang!' and 'Dar she blows!' and finally, blowing indeed and with a good deal of 'ow, danging' on her own behalf, Evangeline was hauled out from the bottom of the boat and triumphantly carried up the beach, two little yellow men to each stout arm and leg, and lots more bent double under her middle. There was a strong smell of scorching as the monster breathed one last breath on the dachshunds' tails, and then it had turned away.

The lifeboat men laid the sacrifice reverently on a large black rock and scuttled like a cluster of huge yellow beetles, back to the safety of their boat.

'Oh, *lor'*!' said the children, uncomfortably. After all, poor Evangeline! But they went on running. Well, they *couldn't* stop – could they?

The monster advanced purposefully upon its prey: and came to a halt. For from behind a rock, out stepped a dark figure, clad in a plaid rug, with

one commanding hand held high. 'Mine, I think?' said the Reverend Tomlinson-Seal; and added with rather less dignity: '*I* saw her first.'

'Mine,' said the monster, breathing fire.

The Reverend looked respectfully at the fire. 'It would save us a lot of trouble,' he said, thoughtfully. 'No rubbing sticks and finding pots and pans and all that.' He looked at the sea-monster, loving him as his neighbour. 'Suppose we settle for that, and share?' Cooked or raw, he added, it was all the same to him; but his dear Mmmmmglummmba-Mmmmm-glummmbans had always preferred it grilled. Medium rare? he suggested, civilly.

Oh, *poor* Evangeline! thought the children. What can we do? And they set up a shrill hubbub. 'A comet, a comet!' they cried in chorus, pointing to the empty sky and the empty sea. 'An octopus, a simply huge, horrible octopus!'

'I don't care for octopusses,' said the Reverend Seal, uneasily, glancing out over the water. 'Nor I for comets,' agreed the monster, rolling in his tongue and looking anxiously upwards. The children redoubled their efforts. 'An octopus! A comet!'

And sure enough, floating in on the waves came a terrible creature of net and straw with tentacles of draggled wet veiling and all covered with lumps of sodden pink artificial roses; and across the moon's face floated a bright object trailing streamers of rich brown false hair.

'Ow-ow,' said Mr Seal, uncertainly, in a somewhat barking voice; and 'Ow-*ow*,' said the seamonster, not at all happily either: ceaseless owow-owing had been coming all this time from the hapless Evangeline, spread-eagled upon her rock. 'If we were very quick,' suggested the monster, 'and didn't fuss too much about the cooking—?'

'Smangle-himble-umbringle-tum-crumblebump,' said the Reverend Seal, which in Mmmmmglummmba – Mmmmmglummmban means, 'O.K.'

A white-coated figure came up to them, quietly. It was the keeper from the aquarium. 'Whatever are you a-doing-of here?' he said to the Reverend Seal. 'You come on back along a' me, to where you belongs.'

'Scrimble-hum-plop-stunk-from-brandlestropping-tum,' said the Reverend Seal, which in Mmmmmglummmba-Mmmmmglummmban means, 'No.'

'Oh, yes, you will,' said the keeper. 'You too,' he added to the sea-monster. 'You'll suit our place fine.'

The monster rolled out his tongue and shot out

a little flame but he did it rather half-heartedly. 'Nothing of the sort,' he said; and together they advanced upon Evangeline.

The keeper said nothing, simply turned his back on them. Across the top of his bald head was written in large black letters: THEN YOU'RE BOTH SILLY OLD FOOLS! He glanced meaningfully out across the dark water and up to the moonlit sky.

Mr Seal and the monster went with him quietly, without another word. Evangeline struggled up from her rock; her usually red round face was now rather white, though, fortunately, as usual practically invisible under her large, round, droopy hat. Sugar and Spice civilly made way for her so that they could run behind and nip Pug; and off they all started again. They ran and they ran and they ran . . .

They were terribly hungry – and terribly thirsty. 'If we could only stop for a minute!' cried the poor children. 'If there was only something to eat and drink!' – and even as they said it, there appeared just ahead, two thin figures standing in a hip-bath – or rather not so much standing as marching up and down with a tremendous swinging of arms and raising of curiously purple

knees; though they appeared to be getting nowhere at all. 'Fiddle! Miss Fizzle!' cried the children. 'What are you doing in that hip-bath?' 'Treading grapes,' cried Fizzle and Fiddle in unison. 'Wine,' cried the children. 'Wine! Give us some wine!' 'We can't stop,' said Fizzle and Fiddle, 'or the jelly-fishes will slide off our heads.' And it was true that on each head was a jelly-fish, delicately wobbling as the ladies soldiered on.

Podge Green came running to meet them. 'Rice pudding, rice pudding!' he cried, holding up aloft a huge pillow-case, bulging with it; and indeed his fat, round face was covered with it too. Even for rice pudding, they would have given all they had; but when they tried to call out to him, all of a sudden their mouths were full of whistle and they could only go, 'Whew-whew-wheeeeeew!' and Sugar and Spice and Pug thought they were whistling to them, broke ranks, advanced upon Podge, who dropped the pillow-case in terror at being set upon by such fearsome beasts and stood aside while they gollopped up the lot. Hardly able to stagger, they resumed their places at the end of the long line of children with Evangeline, Podge Green now with them too: and which of the five wobbled most when they ran, it would be very hard to say.

They came to a sign-post. PUDDLETON-ON-SEA it said, pointing back the way they had come; but the other sign said TO LITTLE PIDDLINGTON and pointed onwards. 'A town!' cried the children, forging wretchedly ahead, their legs hardly able to move, but powering on like little engines, just the same. 'There'll be something to eat and drink in a town.' And sure enough, soon their feet found the hard surface of a proper road instead of soft, white sand and ahead of them they saw the dark outline of houses, with a narrow street running between. But all the windows were blank, like closed eyes, still asleep; and when they knocked at the doors, voices cried, 'Go away! You've got the wrong lodgings, this is OCEAN VIEW, this is SANDYBANKS, this is the HAPPYHOLME BOARDING HOUSE – you've got us mixed up, *you* want LIBERTY HALL . . .'

They caught up with a crocodile of boys, creeping in the dawn, unwillingly to school. 'Join in with the boys,' they cried, all down along the line, 'we may get some breakfast when they reach the school!' But the master came swish, swish, swish with his cane across their stumbling legs. 'Go away, go away!' he cried. 'I know what you want, you want lobster, but you shan't have any, shell-fish is bad for you, you'll see boys before your eyes.' The children could not help rather hoping that the sea-monster was at this moment seeing boys before his eyes after all the crab he had eaten, shells and the lot; but no doubt that would in fact be delicious for him, especially if the boys were fat, so they un-wished it again; and anyway, they had enough to think about for themselves.

They passed a little station. 'A train!' they cried. 'A train will take us home!' And indeed a train was standing in the station, its engine sending up a shower of dancing sparks into the early morning dark. But a voice cried, through a foghorn, 'Allstationsto *Woant*hurt, *L*ystill, *Bee*sick and *Bed*pan . . . All change at *Big*dose, *Little*pill and Wantergoterthe*loo* . . . ' And none of those stations was home. The children had to run on.

Chapter 8

THEY ran and they ran. The sun came up and the hard road grew hot beneath their pounding feet; and when they turned off into the lanes, the hedges were thick and high, closing them in from the fresh morning air. And when they reached out, as they raced by, for the bright fruit and berries that glowed there, or only for a cool flower to lay against their burning faces and bring them a breath of sweet scent – they found that all the berries weren't berries at all, but things of paste and paint, and the flowers weren't real flowers at all, but bits of silk and twisted wire: and the ferns were feathers dyed green and the golden stems were nothing but bits of straw. They were running, running, running through lanes of preposterous great hats. 'Oh, well,' said the children, 'at least perhaps the hats will keep the sun off our poor heads,' and they each seized a hat and clapped it on as they ran. (Yes, well, of *course* they looked silly, a long line of children running along country roads in huge old-lady hats; but it was better than sunstroke. You'd have done the same.)

On and on. The Big Ones in the lead, the Middlings trailing after them, the Littlies trailing after *them*, lugging the Tinies; Podge Green and Evangeline, wobbling along, helping one another, for Podge was somewhat blinded by the rice-pudding on his face, and Evangeline by the floppy round hat. Sugar and Spice and Pug brought up the rear, without even the energy to nip. 'Oh, for some food!' they all cried. 'Oh for something to drink!' Even Podge and Evangeline and Pug and the dachshunds had got over the rice pudding and could have done with something more. Only Miss Prawn's mother was happy and comfortable, munching away at her soap as poor Prawnie, chilblains glowing, galloped along beside the children, propelling the foaming bath-chair.

They came to a village and now the windows were open and lights were on and from the fried fish shop came the most delicious aromas. 'Oh, give us some fish!' cried the children. 'Please, please give us some fish!' And lo and behold! who should appear in the doorway but Mrs Bloggs from the hospital, carrying a great big bucket; and she dipped her hand into the bucket and started throwing fish to them. But as she threw, she began to spin, dizzily, round and round in little circles, quite scarlet in the face with high temperature, and buzzing away happily to herself; and as she spun, the fish flew wide; and there appeared on the far side of the road a huge wooden table and all the fish went flop, flop, flop under the table; and were glued there to the under-side.

And the empty pail rolled out into the road, and to add to her miseries, the wretched Prawn got one foot stuck in it; and clattered dreadfully as she hopped and hobbled along behind the bath-chair. 'We must get her to a hospital,' said the children among themselves, 'and have it wrenched off, if only to stop this terrible noise.'

But at the hospital, the nurses were all tied together by their apron strings, a great octopus mass, struggling to get free: and when the children tried to untie them, running round them

in small circles, each taking a tug at an apron string as they passed, they saw that the hospital was guarded by very fierce animals in cages made of upside-down cots; and that the animals were extremely likely to break free. 'Ow, ow!' cried the children, rather anxiously. 'Help, help!'

'We'll help you, we'll help you,' cried a dozen voices; and a fleet of old gentlemen came surging down the hospital steps. They looked very odd, for some of them were in dressing-gowns much too small, with their poor thin sick legs showing miles of striped pyjama, and some of them in dressing-gowns much too large, stumbling over the hems of them as they ran. But still they were coming to help; only now the children saw that they were tied tight to the ends of their beds by the cords of their dressing-gowns, and towing the beds behind them. And the beds all got stuck in the doorway of the hospital and a terrible traffic jam ensued: and leaping from bed to bed in a sort of tribal dance was a stout old gentleman whose pyjama top flew wide, showing a tummy, dyed to a brilliant blue. But as he danced, he carried on one hand, like a waiter, high above his head a hospital supper tray: and the tray was laden with thick soup, steak and kidney puddings and plum duff.

'Oh, Mr Stout,' cried the children, 'give it to us, give it to us! It's our favourite meal!' But round the corner came whizzing in an invalid chair, an angry old lady, also brightly blue. 'Nonsense, nonsense, give it to *me*!' she cried. 'I've been out for an airing, I'm frozen, I need to be warmed up.' 'Oh, Mrs Chumping,' cried the children, 'we didn't know they meant an air-ring; we were trying to be kind!' But Mrs Chumping only growled at them almost as fiercely as the animals and they couldn't wait any longer, they had to run on.

374

A line of empty cabs came ambling by. 'Rescue, rescue!' cried the children and sure enough the cabs stopped and they all climbed in. But the floors of the cabs had been taken out and they found themselves running as much as ever; indeed the drivers would have whipped up their horses and run the children almost off their feet, but the horses remembered their kindness, perhaps, and refused to move faster. So they all scrambled out again; and when a fleet of bath-chairs caught up with them, they didn't even bother: which was just as well, for the chairs were filled with angry old ladies and gentlemen bleating out for the youth-giving properties of a covering of whipped white of egg . . .

The long day passed – the long, long, weary day: and they had been running since last night, when the stars had come out and sparkled in the deep blue velvet of the evening sky. Now it was hot afternoon; and it should have been tea time, only there was no tea. They thought about the possibility of cake in the hats they had picked from the hedgerows; but the seagulls had thought of that first, and no cake was there. And then . . .

And then . . .

They breasted a hill; their poor tired legs just slowly grinding along like little piston engines, their tummies aching, their throats dry with thirst . . . And there in a meadow on the other side of the hill, was the strangest sight. For it had been snowing. Just in that meadow alone, it had been snowing, and all the ground was white – as white as the tablecloth laid out in the middle of the meadow, laden with good things to eat – with ham sandwiches and jam sandwiches, and every kind of cake; with a great brown teapot in the middle and jugs of milk and sugar-basins heaped high. And sitting all round the picnic, in their good serge dresses and their good flannel petticoats and their high button boots, were Great-Aunt Adelaide Stitch and Mrs Grobble and Mrs Guttziz and Mrs Rumbletum and all the other ladies, wearing each other's hats. 'Oh, Aunt Adelaide,' cried the children, 'oh, Mrs Grobble, oh, Mrs Guttziz, oh, Mrs Rumbletum! – we're so hot and tired and thirsty, do please give us something to eat!' But the ladies sat motionless in their chairs. 'We can't,' they said.

'Can't?' said the children, still running, but running round the picnic now, and the ladies and the chairs, in a sort of Red Indian circle.

'Why not?'

'We're stuck,' said the ladies; and now that the children looked closer they saw that indeed the ladies did seem fixed rather tightly in the deck chairs and in very curious positions indeed. 'The

We're stuck

canvas has slit,' they said, 'and we've all got stuck.'

A sort of vague, vague memory began to come back to the children. Had they not, long, long, long ago before the world was just a place for running through – hadn't they got stuck in those very deck chairs? Hadn't they been stuck there, looking up at the moonlit night, listening to the shush–shush lullaby of the sea and longing to go

to sleep; and staying wide awake . . .? And –
falling asleep at last. But what had they been
saying, just before they fell asleep . . .?

And the children positively stopped running;
and standing in a ring round the picnic laid out
on the snow-y ground, said to one another, their
hot, flushed faces growing pale: 'The Baby! All
this time the Baby hasn't been with us. Where is
the Baby?'

And a voice said, with a shake in it: 'Yes, what's
happened to the Baby?' And a voice said with a
break in it: 'All this time we've been thinking
about our tired legs and our empty tummies –
and forgotten all about the Baby . . .' And a voice
said with tears in it: 'We've been selfish and
beastly, just worrying about ourselves, and never
even given a thought to our own poor Baby . . .'

And suddenly – everything began to happen at
once: for the whole white picnic tablecloth
seemed to have come alive. Cups and saucers flew
up in the air and came down with a crash, cake
and sandwiches flung themselves about as
though, beneath the snow, a volcano had erupted;
the teapot streamed hot brown tea, the milk jugs
streamed cold white milk, the cakes and

sandwiches were split to smithereens. And Great-Aunt Adelaide Stitch rose up and out of her chair and streaked off across the snowy field as fast as her thin old legs would carry her; and after her went Mrs Grobble and Mrs Guttziz and Mrs Rumbletum and all the other ladies, and with *them* went Miss Prawn, clankety-clank with her bucket on her foot, great cries of protest coming from the soap-lathered bath-chair. And Podge and Evangeline detached themselves from the ring of staring children and lit out after them, and Sugar and Spice gave one last loving nip as Pug's curly stump of a tail disappeared after *them*. And a voice said: 'Oh, my naughty children – my wicked, wicked ones! – I was beginning to wonder when you'd be kind again.'

And Nurse Matilda stood there with the baby safe in her loving arms: in her long black skirt and her rusty black jacket and her little black bonnet, all trembly with jet – and her face was so lovely that all the children cried out: 'Oh, Nurse Matilda – how pretty, how *pretty* you look!'

If only it hadn't been for that one huge tooth sticking straight out over her lower lip!

And Nurse Matilda smiled; and she lifted up

her big black stick and gave one gentle tap with it on the snow-y meadow grass. And out flew the tooth and landed in the snow, at the children's feet.

And it began to grow. It grew and it grew. It grew until it was the size of a matchbox. It grew until it was the size of a snuff-box. It grew until it was the size of a shoe-box – of a tuck-box – of a suitcase – of a packing case – of a trunk, of a big trunk, of a simply enormous trunk. And all the while, as it grew it was taking shape; growing tall and curved, growing painted and shining, growing curly painted patterns on the shining paint: growing little curtained windows, growing big yellow wheels, growing shafts, growing a stout brown horse between the shafts, growing little steps up to a little painted door . . . And all the children cried out: 'It's a bathing machine! It's a painted bathing machine!'

But it wasn't: it was a caravan, a gypsy caravan, much, much bigger and brighter and gayer than any bathing machine. And, carrying the baby, Nurse Matilda went up the little steps and ducked through the little painted door; and all the children went in, crowded in, pushing and piling in and yet

each seeming to find a comfortable place with lots of room: all clustered round Nurse Matilda as she sat in the centre of the painted wooden seat, curled up around her, wearily, safely, tired-out from their long, long journey; dropping off to sleep around her, one by one, like drowsy bees in a bright-painted honey-pot. And clip-clop-clip went the hooves of the stout brown horse, and nid-nod, nid-nod went the weary heads . . . And there came a big gate – but it wasn't the gate of the Puddleton sea-side hotel; and a curving drive up to a big front door, standing wide. And smiling down on them were the welcoming, open windows of their own dear home!

And – how could it have happened that to each child it seemed as if loving arms came around him and he was lifted up gently and his weary head cradled against a kind shoulder? And he was carried softly and silently into the house and up the wide stairs and put down carefully in the safety of the dear old nursery-schoolroom at home . . .

And suddenly, they were all wide awake; wide awake and sitting round the big old schoolroom table, with the sunshine pouring in at the open windows – and Nurse Matilda was saying: 'Now you must write your bread-and-butter letter to your Great-Aunt Adelaide . . .' So they clustered round the table and earnestly wrote the letter. 'Dere Great-Arnt Adelaide,' said the letter, 'Thank yuo very much for haveing us to stay at the sea side after we came out of hospidilt . . .'

But when they had come to the end of the letter, and had dutifully sent love to Avangeleen and Pug and Fiddle and Miss Prorn, and had time to look up – the Baby was sitting in its high chair beating cheerfully on a plate with its silver spoon – but Nurse Matilda was gone.

CHRISTIANNA BRAND
(1907–1988)

was born in Malaysia and spent her early years in India. In addition to being a writer, she also worked as a model, dancer, shop assistant, and governess. Known for the lively sense of humour she conveyed through both character and dialogue, Brand herself once said, 'I write for no reason more pretentious than simply to entertain.'

EDWARD ARDIZZONE
(1900–1979)

and his brothers and sisters lived with their eccentric grandmother in Suffolk, England. His cousin, Christianna Brand, was often there too as their parents were all working abroad. The children loved their grandmother, especially for her wonderful stories. NURSE MATILDA was one such story, and was kept for the times when they were really naughty – which was probably quite often. Years later, Brand and Ardizzone would turn it into a book. One of the best-loved illustrators of the 20th century, Ardizzone wrote and illustrated more than 150 books, winning the first Kate Greenaway Medal for children's book illustration in 1956.